Beasties

A Sci-Fi Rock Opera

By Gary Sohmers
©2022 Beasties Universe, LLC

"Book of Grā"

*There are good and bad Beasties
within us all.*

ISBN# 978-1-7362350-3-4 (Softcover)

Library of Congress Catalog Number (LCCN) 2020923593

Any references to historical events, real people, or real places are used fictitiously. Names, characters, and places are products of the author's imagination.

Front cover image by Philo Barnhart, Kathy Wade.
Edited by Tiffany Hulse.
Book design by Tiffany Hulse.

Beasties Universe, LLC
Po Box 702
Hudson, Massachusetts, 01749

www.beastiesrockopera.com

Dedication

This story is dedicated to people who taught me to recognize my Beasties, and to always be involved in evolving a more civilized world of kindness... one perspective at a time.

Acknowledgments

Edward B. and Shirley Sohmers, Thomas Sohmers, Chip Sohmers, Merilee "Merf" Sohmers, Tiffany Hulse, Tia Garbenis, Chris Farlowe, Vivek Tiwary, John Koumoutseas, Bill Holloman, Bill Holloman Jr., Elizabeth Proteau, Mia Moravis, Barrence Whitfield, Melanie Tonia Evans, Philo Barnhart, Peter Bernard, Gary K. Wolf, Bob Eckstein, Elizabeth Falk, Tom Majesky, George Contrada, Rita Mercer, Penny Mills, Ann Reilly Tennes, Dr. Peter Erines, John Lennon, Pete Townshend, Bob Dylan, and Dr. Albert Ellis.

Table of Contents

Introduction

As a child, I was influenced by, and inundated with, the growth of electronic media, and music and marketing—and if I was going to choose a path in life, it was probably a wish to be rich and famous in show business. All children of that certain era whom I knew wished we all could be a musician, dancer, television or movie star, instead of a fireman, policeman or teacher. Show biz looked like the best life because we didn't know that it was scripted, and not reality.

My parents wanted a better life for themselves and for their children (I am the oldest of three), and we had all of the accoutrements of a progressive and affluent family, even though our Dad really couldn't have afforded it on his income. Still, our parents provided. Dad wanted to be in show biz, but knew he needed to provide for his family, so he set aside his own dreams and concentrated on his reality, the choice of which my siblings and I did not understand.

Our TV showed me the world and, even though at times I was merely the remote control for my father's channel-changing needs, I was able to witness history, art, science and mysteries—beyond what my Dad could experience when he was my age. We watched channels grow from four to four hundred. We saw the evolution of pop culture styles in entertainment, including men flying into space, and images of nature in remote locations on the other side of the planet. We witnessed the greatest comedy and scripted drama. The news was never good, no matter how they said it, what with war, politics, and bad people dominating the headlines.

As a teen, I wrote poetry and tried to write songs of teenage angst, or popular themes of silly love, or overly wordy protest. Like most aspiring teens, I liked my own works, but didn't share them with many people, due to embedded low self-esteem about my artistic abilities. My father often told me that I wasn't good enough to be an artist or musician (that hurt), but I held it within.

Sure enough, Baby Boomer that I am was bitten by the bug at a young age, and when I was old enough to strike out on my own, I decided that fame and fortune awaited me at the end of the rock and roll rainbow. I was young, delusional, and completely unaware of how to achieve that dream, but that didn't keep me from making as many mistakes as possible to get the answers.

We lived in New Orleans when it was swinging, moved to Nashville when it was burgeoning into commercial popularity, trekked to Philadelphia during the Bandstand years, and landed in New York when the Beatles arrived. After all that came Chicago, where the Blues lived.

My determination to learn all, and enjoy it, led to meeting musicians for jam sessions, moving their amps, and hanging concert posters and flyers, all of which led to more gigs— not just for the education of it all, as some even paid money! I learned that I had a gift picking new up-and-coming talent, and was lucky to work with many bands who succeeded because of my awareness and assistance.

A particular gig helping an important blues musician taught me to be humble—and working with music businesspeople taught me to be cautious. I landed a great gig as a producer at one of the best concert venues in Chicago, and was lucky enough to help numerous acts gain record deals, connections, and fame. And that is where alcohol caught me.

I then moved to Wisconsin where beer is the state drink. Despite the extreme negative influence of the malt and hops, I was able to apply my knowledge and sales skills to elevate to my next level in the music business, acting as agent, talent representative, and concert producer. I still wanted to perform, write songs, and be a rock star, so I assembled musicians, recorded songs, and performed in a few concerts. I was living my dream, doing all that I wanted to as an independent.

Alas, alcohol consumption led to cocaine use, and both led to severe bouts of anxiety and depression. Despite my "successes," I was consumed by doubt, paranoia, and underlying anger at "reality"—I was convinced that I was perpetually surrounded by bad luck, and that I was making bad choices when presented with good ones. My irrational beliefs were overruling common sense. Was this show biz, or was this self-destruction?

It wasn't easy but, in order to continue to achieve my show biz dream, I reassessed the influences of my younger life. I moved to New York City to concentrate on the pure guts of reality in order to survive and flourish in my dream. I was a big fish in the small pond where I'd lived before; now I was a tiny fish in the Big Apple pond. I was lucky to have show biz friends in New York for whom I'd done favors, and they gave me a few small-time, but valid, opportunities to prove my worth, while I earned others.

Having eradicated alcohol and drug use from my routine, I was easily able to use my skills and knowledge to get a good gig as a stage and road manager, all while keeping up my chops playing and singing low-key gigs with some great musicians. My ego was tamed, I was comfortable, and the music was enough (whereas for many, a status that is always fleeting).

Amidst constantly seeking gigs, I was often hired by producers, promoters, or bands, to fulfill a range of show duties, be it equipment wrangling, security, stage management, counting box office revenue, or escorting talent to a pizza joint. Being able to do it all was indeed an attribute to getting work.

It was no surprise, therefore, when I got hired to be a show producer's stage manager for a free concert in Central Park. I spoke on the phone with the promoter's rep before the show. We discussed my services, and they said I would be assisting the sound crew, keeping an eye security-wise on the audience, and moving equipment when needed.

The best part about this Central Park gig was that the group and the singer were on my list of favorites, and their new record—which I'd already heard and loved for a month—was an exceptional work evoking positive change in human behavior. The music and the messages were inspiring, and I was happy to be able to add my expertise to make sure the concert went off without a hitch. It was to be a professional experience for the band, an enjoyable experience for the audience, and a profitable experience for the promoter from his "sponsors."

I showed up early enough to help the stage and band crew set up the gear, and then went to sit in the grass to decompress prior to all the fun. I thought about the show and where I was to be positioned—stage right to start, near the monitor mix board. The sun was bright and warm, and I watched the squirrels foraging around the empty trash cans and the bases of the nearby trees. The sound of birds singing was all I heard for a few moments.

That was when everything got a little weird…

What you're about to read is what happened next, to the best of my recollection.

And if it was all in my mind, I hope you enjoy the mystery with me…

Chapter One
"Introduction to a New Reality"

Squirrels appear, to me, to be kind of dumb creatures that have no purpose, except as part of the food chain, and watching them brings little amusement. I'm sitting peacefully, observing, as this one squirrel appeared to be observing me. The last thing I clearly remember of my previous reality was the squirrel moving toward me while I was trying to take a picture of it with my mobile phone.

I was hit by a blinding beam of sunlight as the squirrel leaped toward me! Then I felt a chemical reaction, similar to the initial onset of LSD—a short twinge that went through my nervous system like an electrical current. Since I'm no stranger to unusual feelings, I didn't become alarmed, just curious.

Was that blinding beam the warmth of the sun, or the outbreak of a migraine? I closed my eyes to look for "floaters," in order to make sure it wasn't a migraine. Check. There were no floaters, so it wasn't a migraine. What in heck was it?

I thought about what I ate and drank. Maybe I was given a psychedelic drug without my knowledge (which was customary at concerts in my past, and I always dug it). Nope. I only ate and drank what I brought for myself. Check. No dosing, but this feeling inside me was growing, almost like acid was rushing through my veins and nerves, just like in previous self-inflicted trips. Was my imagination expanding? I was always a big dreamer.

Suddenly, I felt complete calm like I was outside of my body, like what happened to me in a previous spiritual meditation experience, but much more complex. Within moments, I sensed that massive quantities of universal knowledge were available to my brain! In reality, that wouldn't be possible. My rational mind attempted to dispel such foolishness. These thoughts *must* be imaginary, I said to myself.

Yet the thoughts strengthened, as did the chemicals rushing through my blood. Within milliseconds, more and more knowledge was stuffed into my memory! Defense mechanisms deep within my subconscious rebuffed the incursion. Was I losing my mind? After all of the experiences in my long life in show biz, though, I sensed that this wasn't going to break me. I am not giving in until I understand more, I reiterated internally.

Then I felt an otherworldly connection within me, like meeting a dear old friend; my innermost fears were subsiding as if a beautifully bonding conversation was rekindled. I closed my eyes really tight, then opened them really fast. Everything around me was business as usual, but within my psyche, I had this newfound belief that some essence, an undefined and uncategorizable impulse had entered my being.

I realized that I was staring into my phone when it happened, and I caught myself staring at it again. Maybe I was hypnotized, or some subliminal technological message was infiltrating my mind, but I couldn't look away. Was my brain wired to some alien internet, wirelessly downloading into my brain everything faster than I could imagine? Yet, I still felt calm and all my anxiety about the effect had already melted away.

I felt as though there were two of me, side by side, operating my thoughts and actions—not in competition, but in tandem. Everything had kicked in so pleasantly, overall, that my psyche no longer resisted (like when the acid was very clean, and gave me a feeling of willingness and happiness, dissolving my ego).

I sat there on the grass, reassessing the situation. Nope. I could be totally wrong. Based on past experiences defining this one, yup. I somehow must have gotten dosed. But, if I am not tripping, I am experiencing something new yet familiar.

And I do know to go with the flow.

Chapter Two
"Good Old Friends"

The professional term among humans is schizophrenic—the combination of multiple personalities in a single person—but I believe that everyone probably has this affliction, so I think nothing unusual of it possibly happening to me.

If not a drug interaction, I will need to accept that I may now have an affliction, feeling like a symbiotic relationship with an invading, yet "cooperative" mental lifeforce. Accepting this potential premise, as I have been able to rationally deal with so many other previous irrational beliefs, allowed me to not fear this. I am, by nature and life experiences, open-minded, but *now* my mind appears to have been truly expanded.

My alien alter ego, whom I refer to henceforward as an "Impulse," appears to have attached his brain to mine, using what he explains is his "pidi"—*personal information and data interface*—and, as best as I can understand, it is similar to a combination of our DNA and our brains. It appears that its goal is to comprehend human emotions, something with which I and so many others continuously struggle.

Impulse, in order to analyze my emotion, in this case my state of wonder, chooses to keep me in this condition; this way, he can also examine my body's chemical reactions to it. He does the same analysis, in barely a moment's time, to numerous other emotions as they are triggered to manifest and subside within me. And Impulse makes time seem to stand still, outside of myself. Although that would be impossible, I sense.

I am just a human and happened to be in this place at this time, as ignorant and unaware of reality as any human, feeling as emotionally insecure as any introverted human, helpless as any depressed member of a manipulated society.

Inside my current combined consciousness, I feel that this Impulse is making me become secure in "who" I am supposed to be, that we have some sort of a collaborative mission, and that all of my experiences and knowledge have led me to handle this very day at this very event. My fear of failure is gone, and my reason to try is clearer. My irrational belief system seems to be modified at a DNA level. All of my previously unevolved fears seem to be removed from my psyche. Somehow, I'm confident that the imaginary voice isn't harmful; it's an old friend.

All of this happened in a blink of an eye. I look away from my phone. The sounds of reality return to my consciousness. Music, people, birds... I am aware of reality, but controlled by my Impulse not to move just yet; Impulse is using all of my senses to get acquainted with my exterior reality. If I'm not tripping, then I'm inhabited. Either way, I am now enjoying it.

Change happened.

An "epiphany" has occurred.

My mind is now wide open.

My instincts kick in, reminding me that I have a job to do, which triggers Impulse to allow me to stand up and return to the rest of the crew, who've finished their breaks, too.

The show is about to begin. I take a few hits off my bowl of weed and observe the band's roadies taking the stage as the audience flows into the concert area. I take my designated position at stage right near the monitor mix board. I'm ready to assist as needed.

Assuming everyone must hear, at least once in their lives, at least one voice in their heads talking to them as they analyze and deduce, questioning and answering themselves in day-to-day decision making, I'm forced to ask myself: Could this Impulse actually be another's voice, and not my own? And how could anyone detect the difference? Free will to believe may be available, but the will to tell anyone else that we *do* believe might be the real dilemma.

I've always felt that people need friends to share their deep shit with, but conversely, I've always been an introverted loner forced into the spotlight of irrational addiction to narcissists. Therefore, I've had or kept very few friends. This sudden shift to acceptance has helped me embrace the small fish in the big pond view of survival, and of actually enjoying life. Now, in this blinding beam-of-light moment, I feel a true friendship to this Impulse.

Impulse moves my hands and my eyes back to my mobile phone. He begins flipping through the various apps, looking for definitions of the words "love," "hate," "fear," "happiness," "empathy," "apathy," and hundreds more variations of the good and bad aspects of thought. All of these words have perpetually confused me, so his investigation will help both of us. These words, I assume, mirror the deep subconscious issues that I've avoided all my life. My preferred words were always "career," "money," "mating," and "ego."

Here at stage right, since there's really nothing required of me at the moment, my daydreaming isn't affecting anyone. Impulse's voice explained to me internally that, from the perspective of the universe, or any other being on the planet that may be observing us from any perspective, *we* appeared, in these past few moments of bonding, to have merely been *a* human looking at their phone. He explained to me that no human outside of us has any idea that an extraterrestrial being is cohabitating my human body, predominantly because of the closed minds most individuals embrace from only existing in human survival mode.

We turn our eyes away from the phone and observe all that's surrounding us. My ongoing commentary from here relates to "us" as opposed to just me, as I now feel bonded with Impulse. At times, I may seem detached, though both bonding and detachment are good for "us," I can tell.

Some of the crew are still scurrying about, adjusting cables and hanging decorative banners. The roadies and tech crew are onstage preparing for the show to start, placing musical instruments in their stands and testing the electrical connections. All of these fellow humans are interacting with gestures and smiles.

I'm thrilled to see such a large number of attendees arriving for the concert, especially since the music and messages are good, and it's a free event. Most people are attending because they're familiar with the band and their newest album, a rock opera that the lead singer wrote for the purpose of effecting change, in mind and action, about climate destruction and the related corporate corruption. They attract an audience of like-minded fans, and this album has become one of my favorites; and I've listened to *all* of their albums. The musical journey of the lead singer, Voice, represented by his lyrics, mirrored my own emotional passage through musical life, but to a different climax. I'm *supposed* to be here now, my new partner, Impulse, assures me.

And I'm not alarmed, at this moment, to discover that my symbiote ability to telepathically hear huge amounts of voices, and accept massive data input, isn't overwhelming to me. I'm literally taking in the knowledge and emotional messages spewing out of the brains of thousands of people as they stream toward the stage!

The general feeling of the audience we're receiving is "good vibes." People have come to share the music, atmosphere, and communal experience in an emotionally and mentally healthy natural state of relief and enjoyment. Impulse and I—we—align with the good vibe. As a duo, we're bonded securely internally. We now think alike, "feel" similar, and are unified, so he's sharing his goal with me to discover the reasons why humans do not care deeply about the survival of the living planet which supports their existence. I no longer believe for a second that this is a hallucination, and consider this now a mission I can assist with to save the planet.

To accomplish this goal, Impulse tells me that we must motivate. Now, I'm able to read minds and to telepathically communicate. I know what people are thinking, and I can see holograms and other bizarre aura mists floating in the air, along with what

I would have previously called *imaginary* creatures, circling around each person.

We're acknowledged by a few of my co-workers with a nod, a smile, a hand gesture, though they're all looking at us with a sense of curious wonder merged with acceptance and security, as is evidenced by these telepathic thoughts I'm receiving. I move to my position, stage right, and it's time for the show.

The band takes the stage as all bands do, the musicians plugging their instruments into their amps, standing in position, and testing their gear, as the audience raise their voices in avid recognition. The band members are Vibe on lead guitar, Bill on keyboards and sax, Sid on drums, and Radar on bass. They've added backup singers for this show. My perch next to the techie in charge at the monitor mix board allows me to hear the same full onstage sound the musicians hear.

Vibe begins the first song, casually strumming the opening chords on his guitar, while walking downstage to front and center, as the audience response grows louder. The singer/songwriter and leader of the band, Voice, slowly walks toward dead center of the stage, strumming his own chords. The crowd is cheering wildly, louder and louder, as the music's intensity builds with the addition of the other instruments. An incredible crescendo ignites the audience even more.

Vibe and Voice, with passion, determination, and finesse, stroke their guitars with the exaggerated windmill move made famous by Pete Townshend. As I stood on the side of the stage, enjoying the sounds of the guitars, Impulse causes me to emulate the swinging arm movements, which I do in unison with the musicians. We appear to now be telepathically tapped into Voice's head.

And since the song was already imbedded in our knowledge from my recent obsession of multiple listenings of the band's current album, I know the melodies and lyrics like I'd written them myself. As he has for many fans, Voice has become my favorite modern poet.

Having always believed that the message Voice conveys through his music and lyrics could change the world into a better society, I sincerely feel that I'm very lucky to have worked my way up through show biz, paid my dues, and am able to be here now. Whether there's an alien inside controlling me, or not, this is a special moment for me—Voice impresses me with his spirit, words, and desire, to effect change. I believe he speaks for us.

We, Impulse and I, are now compelled to be physically excited, and emotionally compelled to smile and feel a sense of comfort in already knowing the song, and believing in the message this musical group conveys. Still standing off stage, but now in view of Voice and Vibe, we're unable to control our reaction to the music. Our body moves rhythmically, and our senses are consumed by all that surrounds us. Whether this figurative acid trip is about to go bad, or if it's all part of the plan, I feel no inhibition because I *know* my place and feel secure.

We're strumming our imaginary guitar, mimicking the movements of Voice and Vibe onstage. It appears as if the universe is aligned, ready for something magical to happen.

On Voice's cue, the music comes to a halt. He stands motionless at the front edge of the stage, poised with his right arm held high in the air, ready to take another swipe at the guitar, ready to create the big noise everyone's anticipating. There's a moment of silence. Everything stops. Even *time* appears to stop. All of the humans, birds, and insects, cease all sounds. The atmosphere is still, just for a moment. It feels as though the entire universe is taking a breath.

In human terms, the moment likely seems like a nanosecond, but Impulse and I are completely aware of the stillness. We scan the mood of the crowd, to take a proverbial *temperature*, and Impulse informs me that the pause is so that if change occurs, it will be supported by science. Our telepathic measurement received a unified *hope* in Voice's messages: Don't just enjoy *life*, but preserve the planet on which *life* exists.

In that moment of silence, Impulse related that Earth is, itself, a living being, and needs to be treated with respect by the humans living on it. Impulse also conveyed that, within this group amassed here at this concert, they appear to be the right ambassadors to effect global human change. Wow!

The very next moment, we *feel* Voice give a telepathic "shout out" to all within his mind's eye! This was something he could only have learned from an otherworldly being somewhere during his evolution, as he is definitely not inhabited by a foreign impulse right now. This moment is pure serenity. Voice and Vibe stand at the front of the stage, motionless, eyes closed, their arms raised in the air, as the quiet rush of wind blowing fabrics, blowing smells atop the breezes, with all of the human senses rendered open and aware, and ready for the next experience in life.

The quiet slowly dissipates as the audience's enthusiasm heightens once more. Shouts and cheers ignite, as chemicals within their individual systems affect each in their own time and manner, triggering mental and physical reactions to their emotional charges.

Upon cue from Voice, all of the musicians on stage attack their instruments like a rhythmic machine, a driving musical momentum, causing the audience to escalate their cheers to a mind-blowing din, and unifying their pulsating movement. The rhythm, which I know by heart, infects me, too, and I begin to move. As I dance, Voice senses our presence. We make eye contact, now reaching a deeper level of telepathic communication between us. Voice and I both believe, I can tell, that telepathic communication is scientific fact. Our minds are now aligned for direct communication, and with no resistance, I dance toward Voice.

Moving toward center stage, I notice a beautiful girl off stage left dancing while painting a poster on an easel. At that moment, Voice's thoughts move from his message to his woman, and we are tuned in. Her name is Terra. We think it's uncanny that she shares the same name as the planet.

My new inner partner seems enamored with her, analyzing and learning about her as the music plays. She seems to float on the stage as she sways to the music, slowly painting an image of Earth from the viewpoint of outer space. Connecting with Terra seems important to Impulse, as if he'd encountered her essence before, as though their basis of communicating is beyond human ritual.

We attempt to communicate telepathically with her, too, but she's so much further into the depths of her own reality that she doesn't respond. She doesn't appear unable or unwilling; her mind is truly open, and there's nothing but pure positivity emanating from her aura.

What causes someone to do something for the first time? To hurtle oneself into an experiment, or life-changing first? To heed an impulse that makes someone do something good, bad, or unusual? At this moment, Impulse moves me to a microphone. I know the lyrics are about to start, and Voice acknowledges with a smile my presence at the mic, as if he's expecting me!

The band changes musical gears, and as I reach for the microphone in front of me, on his special day, at his special event, Voice gestures diplomatically and dramatically like it was rehearsed, allowing me to sing the first line of his first song,

> "Is this just an endless stream,
> Another day get up and dream?"

Is Voice in on my acid trip? Is there an impulse in him, too, or does he just go with the flow, as I do? Our eye contact assures each of us that this is the way the flow goes. Voice then turns toward Terra and sings the next line,

> "In decision, in despair,
> Romantic's life is just not fair…"

It's like this is all completely rehearsed in advance. Terra smiles at Voice. We sense minimal confusion in her mind, even with my presence and my singing Voice's lyrics. Her essence exudes that she assumes this was rehearsed in advance without her, and it is of no concern to her.

Voice looks to me and smiles as I sing the next line,

> "But why must this happen day in and day out?"

Voice's attention stays focused on Terra as he sings to her,

> "Why must my hope always end up in doubt?
> Is my fate just to be some unknown shroud?"

And we all, in unison, sing the next words to the audience, echoing the doubt in Voice's lyrics,

> "I'm not sure."

Vibe joins Voice downstage as they pummel their guitar strings, churning out the power chords leading into the chorus, their minds, bodies, and collective spirit unified as one. This compels Impulse to push me to sing the next line, reflecting the view an outsider attempting to understand the beliefs of another culture would have—*their* culture.

> "If I could see what was wrong with you,

I would understand."

To which Voice responds, again toward Terra—he wants to make sure she understands these words he's written for this song was for *her*,

"If I could see what was wrong with myself,
I'd be more of a man."

When his gaze moves away from Terra to the band, Voice and I make eye contact and turn to the audience and sing together,

"And if I could see what was wrong with this whole world,
I would lend my helping hand."

Voice then points at the audience and sings emphatically,

"And what about you?"

A look from Voice encourages me to follow his lead. I look to the mass of smiling faces, feeling the good vibrations as the music swells, and raise my voice and hand, asking in song,

"What about you?"

In the incredible emotion of this moment, Voice and I lock eyes and sing to each other,

"And what about you?"

We pause. Voice sings to me, sincerely, like we've known each other forever,

"My good old friend…"

The band then kicks in with raucous driving force, led by Vibe's searing guitar, blazing into the wind. The audience swirls excitedly. I think about everything happening in my head, my body, and around us. I have no fear. I have no anxiety. I am where I am supposed to be, doing what I am supposed to do. I have no doubt. This is what my life's mission is all about. Or I'm just trippin' big time.

Yes, it appears that there's more of a connection between Voice and us—Impulse and me—than I could ever have imagined, previous acid trips notwithstanding. But this is my first time in this state of duality, being of sound mind, *and* when I'm pretty damned sure it isn't chemically induced. And even with the knowledge of the universe now planted within my own personal information and data interface—my new pidi—another new-to-me moment about we humans has occurred!

Even though I've relegated myself to my antisocial lifestyle, having given up my egoistic lifelong rock star dream, I'm honored to be singing onstage with Voice, especially in front of a huge audience, *and* accepting that he's truly treating us, I mean me, as a collaborator and friend. Somehow, he even telepathically relayed, with a glance and a smile, mutual acceptance and respect to us.

My Impulse tells me that Voice's music correlates with, and appeals to, a human's vibrational levels of pleasure and thoughtfulness, allowing their constant comportment of sustained discomfort associated with real-life decision-making to be overcome, thereby imparting acceptance of that person as friendly—a complicated way of saying we *can* all get along, and music helps with that a lot. And by "we," I mean my Impulse and me, along with the "we" of the audience dancing with abandon in front of us; we're all *friends*, because we felt that common vibration.

The music is rockin' and I am in the moment, watching Vibe guitar-solo to the enthusiastic crowd. Voice's eyes meet ours, and we feel as if he and we were looking into a pool of water reflecting back to us. Could we be of the same ilk, transcended into different humans, with similar or different missions, to spur evolution, or destroy its progress? Or are we just a cosmic coincidence?

We're strangers who now feel like long-lost buddies. Through Voice's song, which we're singing together, and through telepathy, Impulse is delving into Voice's life in the twenty-first century as a songwriter, a man who loves, feels, and wishes to create, but who lives in an environment of hate and fear, of greed and division.

I turn our attention away from our internal communication and focus again on the masses. The band is actively stimulating the crowd and reacting to their movements. As the song changes direction and the horn section snaps the crowd, the view from the stage is of that of the audience unified in dance, creating the motion of waves.

My eyes move to Terra, spinning and smiling, and Voice dances around her like the Moon around the Earth. As a duo, they flow with the music, their natural magnetic polarity keeping them a proper distance apart. Voice swirls and twirls, then reaches for the microphone with the finesse of a ballet dancer. He smiles at the audience and sings,

> "The earth spins 'round, a day goes by,
> I'm feeling healthy, I don't mind."

Voice gestures toward Terra as she happily rotates in front of her easel. Then with a nod to her (and one to me, followed by a smirk), he faces the audience and sings defiantly,

> "Trying to make another buck,
> This modern world really sucks."

His message is understood by his fans, and they respond with untamed cheers. Voice looks directly at me, and in return, we give him our undivided attention as we sing in unison,

> "But why must this happen day in and day out?"

Voice turns to Terra and asks a second question in song,

> "Why must my hope always end up in doubt?
> Is my fate just to be an unknown shroud?"

Terra, comforting Voice with his own lyrics, as would a friend grasping for the answer to a tough question, offers him a simple,

"I'm not sure."

Vibe steps in between us, guitar slung low, and volume cranked, his anthem of power chords shattering the drama between the three of us. Taking his cue, and with microphone in hand, I join him. And there's Voice, smiling right beside me. The music and the message make my confidence soar!
Again, I sing to Voice,

"If I could see what was wrong with you,
I would understand."

But this time, with the strength within me from my new internal belief system, my newfound knowledge, and an alien-to-me Impulse. And, oddly, I'm responded to by Voice and band with some weird sense of submissive kindness. Voice repeats his confessional desire for knowledge and change, confidently singing,

"If I could see what was wrong with myself,
I'd be more of a man."

Terra, with a vocal prowess all her own, points at me and adds,

"And if I could see what was wrong with
this whole world,
I would lend my helping hand."

And we all sing:

"And what about you?"

She's mimicked by Voice, who's also pointing at me and singing full-throat throttle,

"What about you?"

Then, we all point and shout to the audience,

"What about You?
And You?
And You and You and You?"

Vibe and the band crank the excitement level up past eleven with his searing guitar solo. As he shreds up and down the neck of his guitar, making guitar gods bow in honor, the crowd whips into a delirious frenzy. Terra joins Vibe at front and center, dancing and proudly portraying her work of art to the crowd—a masterful representation of earth viewed from above, with the words "Save The Planet" inscribed beautifully around it.

Voice joins Vibe and Terra and gestures us to join them. The crowd surges forward to meet him, hands reaching toward him, as we all scream to the audience with pure melodic power a gut wrenching,

"What About Yooooooouuuuu?"

Vibe and the band escalate the speed of the song's finale. The guitars are screaming a crescendo of aural resonance mixed with Sid's driving, hysteria-mounting rhythmic frenzy. The song concludes, and the roar from the masses is as powerful as the palpable, thumping wave of vibrations from the full-volume pumping amps. Welcome to the show.

Yes. We are among friends.

Chapter Three
"Forever Girl"

So that was weird. I just joined a band's show—unrehearsed, unprepared, and as an unknown to the band. Something is definitely different. The song. The experience. The bonding. All driven by an Impulse? The audience is cheering for what seems like a millennium.

Time… Here, in five or ten minutes of *time*, all of this has happened!

I don't need to analyze it; it happened and can't be changed. What happens next will be the surprise. So, I will trust my instincts. My gut tells me this unusual Impulse is beneficial to me. My gut has served me well in the past.

So, I will go with the flow… In the here and now, I'm trying to enjoy and remember every moment. It feels like a career dream come true (or a hallucination). Either way, if I'm not assigned anything else for my gig here, I'll go with whatever happens.

I'm feeling a bit anxious, but interestingly enough it has nothing to do with singing in front of thousands of people. Terra's natural beauty, smile, and allure, are causing me to be emotionally smitten, knowing full well that she is unavailable to someone like me. And she inspires me with her singing, art, and desire for positive change in the world. And she's triggered something in my memory.

Despite feeling a bit shy about it, my eyes diligently follow Terra. Her easel is across the stage from me, and she is walking toward it. The music begins again with Vibe strumming his guitar. The melody soars gracefully, completely different in mood and rhythm from the previous song, but emotionally and musically familiar to me as I had listened to this record vociferously upon its release last month.

At first, I was concerned that Voice was shaken by my appearance on *his* stage, in front of *his* band and *his* love interest, singing *his* songs and appealing to *his* audience. Now, he's watching me observe Terra, and I'm thinking he may be trying to figure out if my behavior will continue, or how he'll regain control. My Impulse assures me that isn't *my* issue, and we both relax into Voice's music.

I gaze at Voice. He closes his eyes and sways to the music. Vibe, mid-strum, is definitely wondering who this weird new person is on the stage singing the band's songs. Voice joins Vibe downstage center and strums along.

Now, it feels like my alien Impulse is communicating with Voice and Vibe telepathically, and I'm in on the conversation! I'm motivated to join them front stage; Impulse assures them that I am no threat, that we wish them no harm, and that all is well.

Wow! This is amazing because this is reality happening, really happening! I'm not dreaming! This isn't tripping; this is beyond both.

Voice looks at me with calm and comfort. From his vast career of songs and interviews, I understand his quest to discover the human spirit through his poetry and his music, and we are both lucky riders on Voice's journey today. And Terra is his inspiration.

Terra dances like a flower tossed by the wind—gracefully, smoothly, erotically natural. Impulse taps into Terra's mind and we discover that she was hired as a backup singer by the concert producer, who didn't know about Voice's previous relationship with her. Impulse reveals to me that Voice and Terra were apart for a year before now. Terra seems happy to be involved, and to be allowed to share her art and singing aside Voice's music, and to be sharing their mutual and symbiotic messages.

Impulse pulls me from my human revelry on love and beauty to inform me that Terra, the human woman we gaze upon right now, represents Terra Firma, the planet, to my Impulse. Oh, yeah, she is beautiful, and appeals to my dormant mating need, but I am older and wise enough to disregard unrealistic expectations about companionship. I'm not even in the running for her affection, although it might have been so fulfilling in another time, only realizing this now that I've been allowed inside of her mind.

My Impulse assesses Terra's every move, as our combined brain hurls past my human barriers. She moves in front of her easel like a remarkably familiar light, an uncanny reflection, a shadow dancing in brightness, a crystal that gleams with the presence of a solar flare, all while remaining calm as a gentle warm rain on a perfect summer day, brimming with innocence and curiosity. We were truly in love with her.

She glides atop the music toward the band mates. Voice greets her with a wink and a nod; a *knowing* smirk between them shows me that their bond is sincerely deep, the connection secure.

Unaware of their previous history, all of her thoughts about Voice are now absorbed into my brain by my Impulse.

Terra looks past Voice–directly into my eyes— and sings,

"You are gray."

as if she's known me throughout my entire existence.

"I am if you say I am,"

I musically reply.

And with a smile she psychically conveys an obvious "Of course you are! Look at you!" (Okay, so it may be a dyslexic attempt at my name, but Impulse and I just accept the moniker).

On Terra's prompting, I turn upstage center to view my reflection in the shiny bass drumhead. There I am! My first glimpse of what I look like, being inhabited by an alien! Or this Impulse. Or just a change in my DNA. Terra's correct. By definition, my being appears to be a hue of the color gray! My Impulse's merge with me has caused my aura to change to a shade of gray matching the silvery gray of my hair!

The band begins to flow into this next tune from their newly released album, which I already know so well that the lyrics and arrangements come naturally to me. This next song I know is about a woman, and now I'm seeing this woman, and discovering the connection between her and the lyrics of the song.

Next thing I know, my Impulse urges me to grab a guitar and strum the chords, right along with Voice and Vibe! I'm smiling at the crowd and basking in *the* most special moment on this stage, a moment I'd given up hope of ever experiencing! To be performing in front of thousands of appreciative souls! I'm lost in the chords.... Lost in the swirling harmonies...

Suddenly, I see a cartoonish aura surrounding Terra and Voice. I'm not sure if anyone else can see it; my Impulse informs me that everything is normal, and that I can simply continue to go with the flow. From a scientific standpoint, it's as if Impulse has released within my body my own brain chemicals in order to calm me. My Impulse to relax came from inside, as if it's a physical manifestation of a segment of my irrational belief system changing for the better. Interesting sensation, for sure. If I'm finally becoming aware, able to see things previously invisible, and communicate with others telepathically, then I need to better understand life, and humankind, from this kind teacher inhabiting my system.

Telepathically, instinctually, the entire band knows there's nothing to panic about. Voice is okay with my presence and participation, so the band is, too; they're ready to support Voice, no matter what. He feels secure in delivering the message of his song, and to his love. That's what matters.

Impulse is in charge now, and I'm feeling no anxiety whatsoever about what could happen next. I'm going with the flow again. What could go wrong?

Voice steps up to sing to Terra, and I'm driven by Impulse to sing his words in his stead. Graciously, he nods his approval, while still looking into Terra's eyes. I sing Voice's lyrics as though he and I have known each other for eons,

> "I've known you through a flood of
> lifetimes,
> When I catch a glimpse of the twinkle in
> your eye."

Voice smiles, secure in his acceptance of my friendly prompt for Terra's attention. He calmly sings his next set of lyrics to Terra,

> "You smile with knowledge of my notice,
> And lure me into the comfort of your mind."

Terra sashays to the downstage and stands between Voice and me. The audience's undivided attention is focused on us as Impulse prods me to sing my appeal,

> "I may not have been ready any time
> before…"

Voice proudly responds with his own,

> "But I'm the man I'm supposed to be now."

This is a total split personality moment here! I can sing the words as if I wrote them, yet I know that I'm being controlled by an *otherworldly presence* to behave in this, how you say, *impulsive* manner! From deep within my soul, and powered by this strange Impulse, I passionately sing—directly to Terra—Voice's chorus about the timelessness of love,

> "You are my Forever Girl,
> You're always in my dreams.
> Since time was young, you've been just
> One step out of reach."

Looking into Terra's eyes, as the music plays, Impulse flashes me back through countless lifetimes, showing me the moments in time when those very eyes smiled at me, always conveying a deep connection. To be here now for her has given me the chance to know those eyes again. Vibe manipulates his guitar strings to create a fluid stream of erotic and eclectic sounds, and as the music carries on, my head swirls with images I can't claim to remember, yet seem so clear.

Those eyes have been with me since the beginning of, what can be considered, *time*.

Impulse is, in syncopation with Vibe's playing, filling my brain with knowledge. The formation of the earth amidst the cosmos, the birth, destruction, and rebirth of nature on this science fiction rock, the evolution of the atom from a single cell to a reasoning being, the growth of awareness and consciousness among all multi-celled organisms, the earth's continuing beauty amidst natural and unnatural disasters. Impulse has connected the awe-inspiring universal knowledge of his pidi with mine!

Voice and Terra dance their rehearsed choreography as I beam with my own happiness of being here now. Knowing what I know now. The music soars, then subsides.

Voice may have written these words for his song, but Impulse drives me to convey them with a newly found universal truth within me. I sing,

> "Time makes no limits on imagination;
> We are as old as we want to be."

Voice smiles at me and sings,

> "When you meet someone special over and over…"

I respond with,

> "But each time unable to be complete."

It's as if the lyrics were written for us to sing together. Our banter continues as Voice smiles and leans toward Terra, singing,

> "I believe that she's out there somewhere…"

And I respond, mimicking his moves on Terra,

> "And hope when I find her,
> I'm what she needs."

Voice, feigning that he's perturbed, plants his hands on his hips, then smiles, not at all fearful, conveying confidence. The audience ignites into applause. He and I, eye to eye, in front of the tens of thousands of adoring eyeballs, with music and heartbeats pumping in tandem, turn to Terra and sing from our hearts,

> "She is my Forever Girl,
> Always on my mind.
> Lost and found Forever Girl,
> One step out of time."

The audience cheers with abandon. Vibe blasts another exquisite guitar solo, and the band churns out a chord progression that roars. As if one with the music, I query my Impulse to explain to me why I am here, right now, doing this. Impulse explains to me that every living being here on the premises—and on the planet—is unique, genetically, and in all ways. Due to evolution, tribalism, and other factors, humans divided into groups as a result of these varied and fallacious beliefs.

I now, beyond any doubt, see cartoonish figures that appear to be representing emotions, each acting out the *feeling* they represent. (I remember seeing such shapes when I was younger—and when enjoying the high of hallucinogens).

Impulse informs me that Terra refers to these amorphic entities as "beasties," outward representations of human emotions which control human behavior. I can now see everyone surrounded by their cartoonish beasties. Terra appears to be lifted by hers; she's able to float gracefully in the air as she and Voice dance.

Can the audience and the band see these beasties?

Yes.

Holy cow! I thought a question and Impulse answered me—telepathically! I can hear words from Impulse telepathically... Can everyone?

Impulse conveys to me that these auras are as unique as their owners' emotions, that they're combinations of divergent attitudes and feelings. He tapped into the audience members telepathically, too. Impulse can sense from each human here, en masse, good and bad, strong and weak, confident and fearful, angry and loving. Each person displays multiple conflictions as they exist in this environment; based on their physicality and facial expressions, most are enjoying the music.

Some humans, though they are smiling, are surrounded by sad beasties. Others are smiling, though they are actually angry, and yet others, I can tell, are smiling through fear. I observed these dichotomies until the music led me back to the third verse of Voice's melodic ode to Terra.

Terra elegantly breaks away from dancing with Voice, and takes the lead vocal, singing her heartfelt plea to the universe,

> "Why do I feel like gravity,
> When I only want to be the breeze?"

She sings representing Mother Earth and nature as the dominant factor in all that happens to, and around her,

> "I feel the magnetic pull of something,
> Stronger than the passage of time;
> Two beings entwined in the destiny of
> nature,

Creating art from division so sublime."

She sings to Voice, knowing that he profoundly feels her because he wrote these words,

"Yes I am Forever Girl,
Always in your dreams."

And to me she sings,

"Lost and found Forever Girl,
One step out of reach."

Voice and I look at each other, mutual respect abounding. We sing,

"You are my Forever Girl,
Always on my mind.
You are Forever Girl,
One step out of time."

The music takes flight as the band builds to the end of the song.

I realize currently that almost all of my actions are controlled by my Impulse. And he has powers that control others from within *me*! By using telepathic influence, Impulse is able to get this massive audience to breathe in unison—in and out, simultaneously… Like a giant meditation session.

Their breathing enhances the soft breezes around us, and the crowd is an individual living, breathing body! A unified part of a giant living organism called Earth.

I look out over this mass of humanity. The beautiful, puffy clouds sailing by above them causes the sun's powerful beams to create patterns on their heads. In the distance, outside of this blissfully unique self-contained atmospheric condition, is a dark profusion of clouds covering the high-rise structures surrounding the concert venue in downtown Manhattan.

The music builds and everyone sings Voice's words of optimism and hope,

> "The rays of the sun are making shadows somewhere,
> The rays of the sun are making shadows somewhere;
> It may be sunny here, but it's raining over there.
> The rays of the sun are making shadows somewhere,
> The rays of the sun are making shadows somewhere;
> It may be raining here but it's sunny over there."

As the song ends, the audience bursts into thunderous ovation of appreciation!

From my human perspective, and from my Impulse's education, I see that Terra is a living, breathing human equivalent of what the universe views as a giver of life, a protector of nature, and of the essence of peace in unity. Terra's smile projects pure light around her. She's surrounded by her beautiful aura of characters. Her eyes are slits of enigmatic darkness; her hair is hewed in terrestrial colors of sunlight blonde and golden highlights, exuding earthy energy. She shyly returns to her easel, allowing the band and Voice to reap the applause.

Had I met Terra when I was younger, she would have been the object of my desire as a mate to possess, to love, to share my life. It's obvious that Voice sees her as that now. She possesses every attribute a wise person wants in a companion, and if I were that person, she'd be all that I'd ever need for a happy future as an artist, and as an individual… Oh, well.

Impulse has telepathically permeated her mind, and he assures me that Terra is an empathetic ambassador of the human race, yet is only concerned with, and distraught over, the situation in the environment around her. Impulse, now deep within her feelings, finds that Terra rebukes the hatred, violence, ignorance, corruption, narcissism, and greed, which permeates the society in which she is forced to exist. She sees an illness destroying the beauty of her planet, and that illness is selfish humanity. She hopes for a future of drastically positive change.

Terra's hope appears to be what Impulse is seeking, so why am I the one he inhabited? Why not go directly into her, or even Voice, Vibe, or any of the others, instead of into an old rock and roll hippie? Impulse knows that my query is to him. He conveys that the answer is not obvious, the solution not easy; I'm being forced to *change* first, then assist *others* to change as my repayment for a life of dues just paid to me. Being chosen by the universe to become an Impulse for positive change is not a bad answer!

I feel that I am now aware…

Chapter Four
"Knock It All Down"

A reggae rhythm begins the next tune, a lilting riff that moves with the blowing breezes. I drift deeper into acceptance of this new awareness, and my Impulse's kind control of my new education. I am now able to telepathically delve into other people's minds!

The ability with Impulse to enter Terra's mind is another unique experience for me. I wish I had this skill when I was younger and trying to mate with women and understand better the depth of their desires. In her simple reality, she's complex, just like the planet she's named for, and she holds, more than most humans, innate understanding of singular definitive principles—she accepts her fate, and yet is still hopeful. The Impulse has found within her, though, darkness from a childhood of parental neglect, intellectual stagnation, and abuse at the hands of narcissists.

Terra, like the earth, protects herself and ensures her bodily safety from harmful effects of the outside universe by surrounding herself with the atmosphere. Clouds, any clouds, always make Terra feel secure. They are a blanket for her. She often feels comforted by rain, too; it soothes the misery she experiences from the anger and fear in her midst.

While in her mind, Impulse and I discovered that Terra's terminology for these cartoon character auras are her "beasties." She identifies them as her positive and negative emotions. As difficult as it is to do at times, she's decided that she must nurture the good ones, and control the bad ones, in order to live a happy life.

Within Terra's senses, we find that a fear beastie seems to permeate all, and it's shadowing her hope. She's like me—an antisocial introvert—and she prefers to be alone, surrounded by nature, animals, and art, with music playing, and she would likely have avoided a crowd like this. That said, she's happy to have this gig as a singer and an artist, and feels comfortable as part of the show, even though she and Voice have a history.

Terra's thoughts of Voice allow us to learn about her connection, since childhood, to him and his best friend, Vibe. Both Voice and Vibe have always been very respectful of her, so she felt, and feels, comfortable at their gigs. Vibe, the practical, factual, technical member of the entourage, who's relatively apathetic about all the *causes* Voice writes about, lives for the applause resulting from his screaming guitar solos and emotional notes; he loves to make audiences swoon, and to see his bank account grow.

I'm snapped out of my thoughts of who-what-and-why when Terra takes me by the arm, grabs Voice by his, and glides us across the stage in step with the reggae rockers riffs. Voice and I look at each other, go with the flow and, haplessly shrugging acceptance of the friendship, lock arms with Terra.

We merrily dance across the stage, each of us humorously employing a faux tug-of- war on Terra, pulling her one way and the other. She laughs. Her mirthful beasties are overwhelmingly evident to me now. She leads us toward the side of the stage, where her easel stands at the ready for her next expression of art.

Voice has invited his reggae friend to sing the next song.

> "Went down to the park, stayed until it's
> dark, had a good time."

EarthaMom sings to the reggae groove as the audience dances in a sea of bobbing heads.

> "Shufflin' with the band, wavin' to the fans,
> winds starts blowin',
> And Jah mon, she can knock it all down,
> knock it all down.
> Go on!"

I am now aware enough to maintain the visual image of every audience member's beastie. I see a fear beastie, running rampant and permeating the crowd. Here among the joy, beauty, and splendor of the musically enraptured human spirit, hope, cheer, happiness, and communal love, in the loving arms of Terra and Voice.

Where is this fear beastie emanating from? What impulse could possess anyone *here* to cause what's wrong with earth, humans, and nature?

Right here, right now, there's a universal human communion of movement, togetherness, peace, and harmony. Among us all, this sound and rhythm is understood as a positive vibration that creates positive energy. The movement of these human forms, with their breathing circulating the atmosphere…we're all rustling with the trees above…Voice and I, arm in arm with Terra, holding the most beautiful woman in the world for only a moment in time, and it's heavenly!

But Terra's face turns to shocked confusion, and she freezes in place. At first, I think she's looking directly at me, but she's staring past me. My eyes follow her gaze, and my senses turn me towards a small group of self-proclaiming (I see by the signs they're carrying) "righteous citizens" pushing to the front of the stage, provoking agitation among the previously unified audience. Their motive is to impart their "message" to Voice's audience, whether the crowd or band wants it or not.

As if that's not enough, the "citizens" are met by a group of self-proclaimed "radical punks" with their own slogan signs. Loud and unruly vibrations disrupt the citizens, who are clamoring for attention. Both groups now move erratically, dancing in an exaggeratedly disjointed manner, out of rhythm with the reggae music's groove. By now, they've all shoved their way to the front of the stage. As the crowd of happy hippies move out of their way, these citizens and punks, replete with fake smiles, push and shove each other, thrusting their signs—their cardboard slogans—into the audience members' faces.

This causes Terra to tremble from fear created by the *cause* of the protests—she doesn't fear the voice of the people; she fears the reason the voice of the people is so fearful and angry. Here, she'd been creating art on her easel, for the audience, as part of the show, for the sake of communicating a positive message endorsed by Voice.

These citizens and punks are attempting the same thing, but in a devisive manner. This is not their party.

The placards in the citizens' hands cite "positive" messages for evil deeds, such as "Dick T.Raitor for Ruler of Earth!," "Capitalism is a Great Ism!," and "Money Talks, Bullshit Walks!" The punks' signs profess their causes of action as, "End of the World as We Know It," "Stop Corporate Corruption and Climate Destruction," and "Destroy Greed to Save The Planet."

The mood of the humans—myself included—is immediately changed from happiness and hope to fear and distrust. I'm personally feeling angry, even without an Impulse, as I have a long-standing resentment toward polluters, bullies, corporate and political corruption, and those who take advantage of innocent people. Impulse informs me that we have now discovered the dire cause of perplexity in humanity *and* the living planet.

These purported citizens' signs convey messages of hate, division, fear, and that greed is good. The punks' messages comport anarchy, change at all costs, and recognize that evil is bad.

I'm thinking we've always believed in going with the flow, so let's see where this goes.

In the second verse of the song, EarthaMom imparts Voice's lyrics about the disparity of political opinions of the current day, the hate spread by politicians, and the revolution called for by radicals,

> "Hate, mon, a really deadly game;
> Players are insane politicians."

Both the citizens and the punks cheer, believing this applies to the evil opposite group.

"Together we can find a way;
To see a brighter day in our future."

EarthaMom sings to the cheers of the kind and loving audience,

"And Jah mon, she can knock it all down,
Knock it all down,
Go on!"

EarthaMom transmits hope for happiness to the crowd, surrounded by happy beasties, grooving to the music—including my own beasties!

I slowly move away from the audience toward Vibe and the band. Terra and Voice approach their microphones downstage next to EarthaMom, and join in singing,

"Now I'm learning, yes indeed, to be patient, and believe,
That a time may come someday, my friend, though we may never see it.
With the grace of Jah, the sun will shine on, and the tunes go ever playing."

The band bangs a lilting riff that gets the whole crowd moving as one again. Even the citizens and punks move in rhythm with the mass of humanity surrounding them. All are breathing, in and out; all expelling carbon dioxide to benefit the atmosphere, plants, and living planet; all together as one, creating movement in the atmosphere.

I assume that my Impulse is somehow psychically causing this. Now, with all in the flow, no doubt or anxiety exists. The very winds themselves embrace the motion breeze created by the people, and pick up momentum, causing the flags and fabrics onstage to unfurl and dance, as though with minds of their own! To her surprise and delight, a strong gust elevates Terra. The stage crew, including me since that is my job, are aware of the winds and ready to batten down the stage if needed.

Voice and Terra dance with EarthaMom, all the while keeping a watchful eye on the two opposing groups aggregated in front of the stage. The audience subdues the boisterous activities of both groups by swarming the front area and dividing the opposing forces.

But right here, in front of the band, the audience, and the universe, the citizens attempt to demean the punks', the fans', and the band's message. Using their signs to block people's view of the stage, and dancing spasmodically, they act as bullies, and attempt to win over the audience.

This type of arrogance I personally just can't stand. They're behaving like this for no other reason than they consider themselves superior to others who do not agree with them.

Impulse tunes us into the citizens' minds in an attempt to telepathically garner their thoughts. Their minds convey the sad message that to push, beat, bribe, or *kill* their way to their goal is allowed. Their internal damaged and irrational belief system emanates narcissistic, materialistic, and selfish behavior. Wow! I can read deeply into their minds. I've met some shitty human beings in my time, but I've *never* witnessed such pathetic people at *that* core belief level.

Toward the end of the instrumental interlude, the punks move into the front edge of the stage—fist-pumping, sign-waving advocates for their messages. The Impulse telepathically links with this mass of mindsets and discovers that they are unified in support of Voice's lyrics and songs, and oppose the citizens direction, but their irrational beasties can cause them to act irresponsibly.

EarthaMom steps up to the microphone, and the punks jump about madly in a frenetic display of overzealous appreciation, ready for the final verse. The audience knows the lyrics EarthaMom will chant are about the punks,

> "Punk mon, really state of mind;
> Players want some kind of revolution.
> Together we can find a way,
> To see a brighter day in our future."

Terra and Voice are at their mics, and I feel compelled to join them. We three join EarthaMom in singing the chorus,

> "…and Jah mon, she can knock it all down,
> Knock it all down,
> Go on!
> Jah mon, she can knock it all down,
> Knock it all down,
> Go on!"

The audience, unified, sings the chorus as the music builds. The lyrics put society on notice that Jah, a/k/a Mother Nature Earth herself, can destroy humanity as easily as she built it.

The sound of thousands of voices singing from their hearts and minds, sending a huge energy force upward, strengthens the wind itself. It grows stronger and stronger as the chorus builds, and the tall trees bend. The sound system stacks themselves would blow over had the stagehands not been there to brace them!

Terra smiles broadly, caught by her happy beasties, as another gust lifts her from the stage. As the song concludes and, as if due to Terra's desire, the breeze subsides, drifting her back to the stage. The roar of the audience is an energy force all its own.

"Knock it all down!"

EarthaMom sings as if Mother Nature's appointed spokesperson for her natural powers. Humanity must remember that, despite whatever they create, Jah can topple it in one fell swoop.

My Impulse reminds me that some humans in the crowd can't fathom the concept, and remain static within their corrupted, unevolved mindsets. I feel sympathy for people of such ignorance. I always try to educate when I can, though seeing their emotions portrayed as childish cartoon-y characters is weird and reminds me of the futility of teaching such people. Oh, well… For now!

As the audience cheers, EarthaMom waves and walks to Terra's easel.

The picture of planet Earth she drew before now has new lettering added...

SAVE ME!

Chapter Five
"Even the Cool Succumb"

The audience is definitely ready for more music! As EarthaMom leaves the stage, Vibe slides to the front to begin the next song. His guitar strings glow in the sunlight, his hands move masterfully up and down the neck. He shreds out what he's known for—a powerhouse wave of energy on his axe, and the band picks up the beat and drives the rhythm home. The punks, and the rest of the fans, headbang in unison as the volume cranks up. Vibe triggers a release of adrenaline into everyone who hears his sound, and this audience is no exception; they're really excited to see and hear him play.

Just out of sight of the band, the *citizens* are aggregating off to the side of stage right on a small platform, decorating it with their signs and banners, all of which was previously undisclosed to Voice. It looks like they're copping this vibe and surreptitiously setting up their own parasite event! The thousands in this audience came to *Voice's* free concert to hear and see *his* band. These citizens are seriously infringing! Even before encountering this all-knowing Impulse, I discovered that distraction is the most common enemy of conscientious awareness. I know what these citizens are up to and it's not good.

Voice and band, ignoring the citizens unauthorized encampment, play on with wild enthusiasm. So far, their adoring fans are still rapt with attention on Voice, Vibe, Sid, Bill, and Radar. Though my body, and my ears especially, are attuned to the sound emanating from the stage, Impulse is honing in on a strange thought path exuding from the citizens, who have completed decorating their platform.

I turn around and espy a sudden flurry of activity. Numerous men, wearing black suits and dark glasses, have entered the premises. Their expressions are stern, and they're all surrounded by fearful beasties! They escort an overweight man in a rumpled suit onto the platform; this man's surrounded by myriad evil and treacherous beasties!

They don't appear to be involved with the citizens' parasitic event, though no one was paying much attention to their activity until a big banner was posted which read, "Dick T.Raitor For CEO of Earth." That was noticed only by the punks, at first, who reacted by throwing food at the citizens.

The punks want change at any cost, and aren't opposed to imparting violence against any person, group, or faction who stand in the way of their progress. The punks, to no surprise, and despite their positive desires, are surrounded by angry and hurt beasties; their slogans convey the mistreatment of humans and earth by the ultra-rich led by Dick T.Raitor and his sycophants, who are clearly hell-bent on destroying evolving civil humanity.

I sense the ever stronger telepathic divide among the fans, who are increasingly confused and angry about the intrusion of the citizens and the messages on their signs. Others are meekly accepting the infringement on their time and space, and concentrate on the band and their music.

Impulse and I feel another essence. Doesn't anybody wonder who paid for this free concert, and who's to gain from it? We have all become so mindlessly ready to be manipulated by advertising and sponsorships in the media, we can sense that the crowd doesn't really understand any of the citizens' purpose, or their goings-on.

Oh, no! We sense that many audience members are now thinking that Voice may have sold out and is, at least for this free event, acting against his own messaging and possibly being corporately controlled! Even those who fully comprehend Voice's messages of the planet's need for sustainability still choose to remain clueless to the dichotomy of that thought path; that way, they don't have to confront, be confronted, or engage outside their comfort zones. *Music matters!* even if rational thought may not.

The band is about to sing again. Voice has invited another friend to join him onstage. Special guest vocalist, PunkHead, joins the band downstage center and grabs the mic from Voice's mic stand, and sings with screaming intensity and conviction,

> "I've got too many irons in the fire;
> A heart filled with genuine desire.
> My brains ain't fried, and I never lie.
>
> "I've got a soul full of true compassion,
> Though it never really seems to be in fashion.
> I can't deny that the time is right."

Voice's words inspire the punks and all of the fans, who dance with reckless abandon to the driving rhythm of the band. PunkHead continues,

"Gonna rock ya, gonna roll ya, gonna really take control yeah!
Gonna move ya, gonna groove ya, gonna really cut ya loose!
I'm gonna be so hot that even the cool succumb!"

Reflecting back on an interview with Voice that I read several years ago in a fan magazine, he'd stated that when he wrote these particular lyrics, he was seriously concerned about the rising temperature of the earth, the melting of the polar ice, and the hierarchy created by the wealthy in an attempt to divide and control the masses. Voice felt that, although *cool* was a term for *smart* and *liberal*, anyone can claim to be however they choose to define themselves, without needing to live that truth. He said that many people may have felt that they *were* cool people, but the reality, in Voice's opinion—and in his music—was that they had succumbed. He said Earth might be losing its battle for survival and, currently, more and more people were less and less educated, and that lack of education meant less people were capable of participating in solving those problems.

In the here and now, at this concert, clearly the citizens want change, too. And now I realize who that sloppy, overweight man is! They've brought their reprehensible corporate political candidate, Dick T.Raitor, to represent them in this unauthorized, steal-the-spotlight rally. Ugh! T.Raitor is the epitome of the evolution of the bully.

Suddenly, I notice two guys off to the side of the stage. They're plugging in long cables into our sound system! The cables stretch from the main stage to the citizens' platform. Now that sloppy overweight man's holding a mic. As though he's rehearsed this moment, he moves in time, and hums in tune, with Voice's music. This fat bully's booming, raspy timbre rattles the amp stacks with total infringement as T.Raitor sings,

> "I had a hard time finding my direction;
> When I looked at my reflection with tired eyes,
> And it's no surprise."

Impulse taps into Dick T.Raitor's brain. We quickly discover that, as a child, little Dick was abused by his family and friends. This screwed up his life, his ego, and his sense of importance, developing a psychological ailment known as narcissistic personality disorder.

I can see them clearly now. T.Raitor's surrounded by hate, fear, arrogance, and greed beasties. Despite that, Impulse and I can easily sense that he's singing Voice's words with utmost sincerity.

> "I make the most of life with what I'm given,
> Though it's hard to believe I could be driven,
> By greed and pride, and not guiding light."

Wow… T.Raitor's trolls have highjacked the sound system, and now Voice's own words! And much to the surprise of all, Voice, though, lets

T.Raitor continue. In fact, Voice *urges* the band to continue playing.

T.Raitor continues singing, musically responding to PunkHead that *he* was…

> "Gonna take it to the limit, better watch me every minute!
> Gonna learn it as I live it, gonna burn it if I wish it!
> Gonna be so hot that even the *cool* succumb!"

Voice's lyrics are about freely smoking marijuana. But T.Raitor is using them to convey his power to force the change *he* wants. He will probably destroy the planet if he gets his way or not. T.Raitor espouses to the crowd,

> "I can't really show you by example,
> Cuz I don't really seem to have a handle,
> On winning ways, just financial praise."

PunkHead vociferously replies,

> "Some people's future is well-written;
> Other people's destiny's well-hidden."

T.Raitor shrugs, and answers simply,

> "Do what you know…"

PunkHead snidely quips in return our *get along* reply,

"Or go with the flow."

T.Raitor proclaims to his followers,

"I'm your fearless leader!
You don't really believe me."

PunkHead retorts,

"Rock and roll's your teacher,
If you let it reach ya."

Each try to out-bellow each other, singing,

"Be so hot that even the cool succumb."

PunkHead overwhelms the audience with his delivery of Voice's lyrics, and a stage-dive into the crowd. The mob cheers with unrestrained glee. Vibe and Voice, both downstage center, expertly slay on their guitars as the rocking crowd swells toward them. The happy mob moves in a cohesive wave of power, outshining completely the group of T.Raitor's citizens and suck-ups.

Dick T.Raitor's narcissistic messages of hate, greed, and fear, echo with zest via his T.Raitor trolls and sanctimonious citizens. It's no secret to Impulse and me that they all hope to benefit from this notorious association with their bully leader. None of these sheeple ever understood history, or evolution (how could they, having never evolved?).

Vibe's solo rips the air and trips atop the wind. This interlude provides Impulse and me with a few minutes to process all of this new information, and to continue our observation. The beasties surrounding T.Raitor's crowd are still predominantly fearful ones, but we can tell that this crowd's sheer numbers are beginning to exude new beasties… Irrationally fearless ones!

The citizens' new beasties appear to be *judgments*—of other people, and of society and science. The citizens are encircled by auras of disgust, hate, greed, and narcissistic beasties, which define the citizens' commonality of unsound belief systems. The citizens can choose to be close-minded because it suits them. They now have support from others who feel as they do, willing to be led by a man who extols these bad behaviors. Birds of a feather flock together.

Voice also sees these new beasties occupying the audience; beasties which, until right now, Voice would never acknowledge to Terra. He looks at Terra and me. We all see the same vision—zillions of beasties dancing with mad wantonness to the band's thrilling music.

Impulse is telepathically sending positive messages to everyone and conveys to me that this is a *mission* from the universe to convince humans that these beasties are real, destroying the planet and in need of deep understanding by their owners.

It's Impulse's attempt to save humanity from destroying itself.

The song revs up with Vibe's notes pummeling the audience, and it concludes with Sid's crashing cymbals.

The citizens and the punks have separated.

Dick T.Raitor has been swept away by his minions.

A stagehand sets a second easel next to the one Terra's using.

Impulse compels me toward the second easel. He makes me draw a meteor streaking toward Terra's drawing of the planet Earth.

Chapter Six
"Stand and Fight"

Impulse explains to Voice, Terra and I that we are now amidst a volatile situation. A group of antagonistic beasties are controlling easily manipulated human beings.

Humans all have discerning brains with the capacity to absorb vast amounts of information— more than ever before in the Earth's history and, in part, due to the internet providing instant gratification for the acquisition of more reality-based data.

That said, though, humans are choosing to embrace an *irrational* reality. I have observed this to be true, whether it be due to input via previous alien thought, i.e., my open mind, or more-so now via my discovery of how an Impulse can impact decision making.

It's further explained to me that the beasties of hate, fear, greed, and narcissism, control a *minority* of humans, but those whom they do control are very forceful, bullying about getting their way. The art of bullyism was, over thousands of years, crafted by humans for the sake of survival, and for control of the tribe's weaklings. Bullies are stronger when aggregated so they can hide individuality within their crowd.

Many of these citizens before us tonight have been led astray; they possess underlying goodness, and Impulse informs me that, if their internal triggers can be switched to a new operating belief system, we can override their falsely frightened subconscious.

They may be able to tame their bad beasties, and music may be the perfect path to do so.

I turn my attention back to the concert. Having listened to Voice's new album numerous times, the set list taped to the floor cites that the band's performing the exact same track order as on the album, so I know what song is next.

The audience feels completely comfortable, nodding away to old-timey, country swing and sway of the song's intro music. If the music is safety for enough of their tortured souls, maybe Voice's message will get through to their failed belief system allowing change to happen.

Voice has been wandering the stage, grabbing musical moments with each of the band members. He roams to center stage. These next lyrics are pointed; he wants to persuade the audience to think differently.

> "You should know by the tone in my voice,
> Life is giving you a multiple choice."

Voice sings in a down-homey twang that even vilest trolls can savor,

> "And I can read what I want into anything.
> Is it real, or am I just imagining?
> Could it be reality or fantasy?
> Just make it critical or flattering!"

His subtext is that anyone can believe anything they want about language, honesty, emotions, or even imaginary beasties.

"Cut me to pieces, build me like a wall!
I want to know how you feel - I give you my all.
Doesn't really matter if I'm wrong or I'm right;
I just want to know if I should run, or stand and fight."

Voice sings with such emphasis that his words immediately ring true to the citizens pumping their fists, right next to the punks pumping their fists, right next to the hippies pumping their peace signs, as the chorus proclaims,

"Stand and fight! Stand and fight!
I won't run away from my guiding light,
Stand and fight! Stand and fight!
Like a king for his queen cuz he knows he's right."

The citizens assume Voice is encouraging them to fight *for* Dick T.Raitor, and the punks take it as Voice's urging to fight *against* Dick T.Raitor,

"Stand and fight! Stand and fight!
I won't run away from my guiding light,
Stand and fight! Stand and fight!
Like Tarzan for his Jane protects her paradise."

I saunter to the beat across the stage to Terra, who's dancing alone by the easels. I join her dance, and we enjoy each other's company while watching the frolicking mass of humans and beasties. Voice's song unifies the audience, though Impulse and I can see that the individual groups are emotionally divided by their beasties—their belief systems.

Voice dances his way to Terra and me and positions himself between us. He dances her to downstage center. Still singing in his traditional country music drawl, he woos her,

> "I can tell by the sparkle in your eyes that subconsciously,
> You're trying to entice me."

Terra is clearly attracted to Voice's courting. He is not only an incredibly compelling vocalist, but she knows he is truly a man of his word, and she's basking in his eloquent profundities which she sees, right before her very eyes, capturing the human spirit of each and every audience member. Voice is the definition of poetry and song! She smiles as he sings to her. Impulse and I see vivid beasties of love and hope circling around Voice and Terra as they dance together.

As Voice reaches the final chorus, he reiterates his message of choice—to believe what you want, and to filter out the false.

> "I hope the girl in you is ready to be a woman,
> Cuz the boy in me is ready to be a man.
> I can read what I want into anything.
> Is it real, or am I just imagining?
> Could it be reality or fantasy?
> Just make it critical or flattering!"

Voice hopes the audience can see that the simplicity in such choices will help them to evoke change in their minds and actions. But he's singing to *humans* themselves, not to the beasties controlling them.

> "Cut me to pieces, build me like a wall!
> I want to know how you feel - I give you my all.
> Doesn't really matter if I'm wrong or I'm right;
> I just want to know if I should run, or stand and fight."

He sings to the masses, as if laying himself on the chopping block, for the sake of change, and to convey to them his own willingness to be vulnerable.

Everyone onstage and in the audience is singing along, their collective volume matching that of the instruments booming through the loudspeakers!

> "Stand and fight! Stand and fight!
> I won't run away from my guiding light.
> Stand and fight! Stand and fight!"

Voice answers with his commitment to Terra,

> "Like a king for his queen cuz he knows he's right."

The crowd yells out,

> "Stand and fight! Stand and fight!

I can't run away from my guiding light.
Stand and fight! Stand and fight!"

Voice sings again his mating call to Terra,

"Like Tarzan for his Jane protects her
paradise."

The intent of Voice's lyrics, "Stand and Fight"—about protecting earth from destruction, and humanity and civilization from extinction—aren't landing with some of the audience members. Instead, the words have incited several irrational beasties, which propel their humans toward physical violence! The previous musical unification is again fragmented.

This causes me to wonder if Voice's attempted universal consciousness thing is above his, or my, figurative pay grade. Voice, nonetheless, is more interested in going with the flow, which is *really* flowing now. That said, it's clear that he and Terra are dismayed at the failure of Voice's musical appeal to soothe these savage beasties.

With their message clearly misunderstood, Voice and Terra witness that the factions in the audience believe their respective way is the only way—the beasties are standing and fighting alright—with each other! They're not prompting their humans to stand up for a proper cause for a rational reason.

Impulse is very concerned that humans might be losing the fight they so desperately want to have because they do not know their real enemy.

They are completely controlled by their beasties…

Chapter Seven
"Beasties"

As "Stand and Fight" draws to a close, a drum beat continues, creating a lush bed of sound. I think to myself that it resembles a human heartbeat. The audience of fist pumpers slowly disentangle themselves and divide into different areas.

Voice and Terra are standing by the easels, surrounded by their beasties of hope, empathy, and kindness. A few of Voice's beasties of concern and worry are also circling. Terra is gazing toward a group of wild and domestic animals, in a fairy tale kind of moment—dogs are chasing squirrels, and birds playfully swoop down and soar upward. I'm not quite sure if Terra is actually able to *communicate* with the animals and beasties, though I'm compelled to wonder if I'm imagining that she is.

Impulse informs me that he has decided to take matters into his own control. As it's explained to me, *time* itself is only a way for humans to understand their reality, but in the reality of the universe, an evolved and transcended entity, such as the Impulse currently inhabiting my body, has the ability to slow or stop the progress of time—it does this by connecting a large group of humans into a telepathic neural web of influence, a process similar to hypnosis.

Impulse further explains some science to me. By sending a unified message to the frontal lobe of the brains of all humans in attendance—a message through which the human parasympathetic nervous system can become accessed and activated—my

Impulse has penetrated the mass of humans' nervous systems. The brain waves slow to the theta range, and allow reality time to, in the humans' minds, slow or stop.

Impulse has stopped *time* in our reality. Every human is still. The atmosphere continues, as does all of nature surrounding the humans. Impulse's message has reached *only* into the thousands of human brains before us. But with the entire planet tuned in to this happening through the internet continuing as before, unaware of this lapse of linear time here and, since time is based on awareness, only those humans in attendance may not be aware that anything unusual happened to them when time begins again.

My Impulse's pidi explains to my brain that, within the human subconscious exists a conditioned being that controls actions and reactions based on the human's past experience. Impulse also tells me that genetic encoding and strength of character develop via the obstacles of *being* human. This is the human subconscious, a place where the beasties evolve and learn to control their human's beliefs and behaviors.

I can now recognize that the good and bad beasties existing outside each human are a visual representation of human emotions. These beasties manifest based on lessons and knowledge gained by experiencing life from birth until now. A human child has instincts embedded within their genetic DNA, within each atom's own individual pidi, and those atoms aggregated become the person. And each person must learn to control their own beasties' behaviors through internal and external growth. But the mind is an incredibly powerful tool, and weapon, to create ideas and feelings—that creation of which is often beyond the ability or desire of humans to understand or control.

It appears that all atom-based beings oftentimes have uncontrollable subconscious manifestations that appear to be driven by good or bad beasties and, at times, can go askew, thereby causing anxiety. It may be caused by outside influences—parental, societal, environmental, educational—and can usually be explained on a human awareness level. The worst beasties are the ones which can't be easily identified; the ones who take advantage of a human, from *within* the human, and the human doesn't even know it!

The heartbeat-drumbeat still permeates the Park, its echo floating in the stillness. With a blink of my eye, Impulse opens only minds of the people onstage, while keeping the minds of the audience in an unaware state.

The beat becomes stronger, and everyone begins to chant,

> "Beasties! Beasties! Beasties! Beasties!
> Beasties! Beasties! Beasties! Beasties!
> Beasties! Beasties! Beasties! Beasties!"

Upon Impulse's prompting, PunkHead awakens from his trance. He recites Voice's poetic words directed telepathically as Impulse transmits into his head,

> "Beasties believe in endless pleas, a tease to ease their freakasies;
> Rants beyond the eyes of dawn;

Comes alive on seeds of song."

A cryptic message conveying that the beasties can be deep and dark emotions,

> "Creepy empty space in time delineates my aching rhyme;
> Sometimes heated sorrow becomes true bliss."

This message conveys change is possible from dark to light.

Terra and Voice respond about their own fear and hope beasties, singing,

> "Even if I've tried to find a pathway to a better clime,
> If my try seemed vastly dark, no glimmer of light, no sign of a spark;
> Even though I feel the pull of every bad decision culled,
> Between my spirit's dream untold,
> I believe there's something to this."

Now Impulse informs me that it's our turn to add that knowledge of human failure can be the root of bad beasties. I join in, singing,

> "A beastie is not just human, psychically diminished ruin,
> Devoured through and through in darkly depths within."

Impulse and I add that the bad beasties blame themselves and their human for they consider themselves...

> "Failed like a withered blowhard, delinquent emotional shit-hard,
> Lost in a ghastly brain fart, disgusted that it's so hard."

I realize that the abuse is self-sustaining to the beasties, *and* to their humans.

All onstage have opened minds and can see the beasties, because nothing within them tells them that these visions are false. Beliefs can change. Some people can see things that others cannot; much like reading music, and solving complex mathematical problems, understanding is about *believing*.

Everyone onstage is aware and able to visualize what Voice and Terra previously thought was only in their imaginations. The bad beasties representing hate, fear, sadness, anxiety, anger, greed, suffering, malice, arrogance, self-centeredness, and narcissism, start behaving as though being called "bad" is a positive thing! They're celebrating being recognized, and they're encouraging bad behavior. Bad beasties *love* a closed mind.

PunkHead begins the second verse, rhythmically chanting,

> "As the art flows through your heart,
> coloured by dissenting marks,
> Leaving space to be replaced by moments of un-splendored grace,

Contradictory desire, contorting even arts
inspired,
No one believes they can change this."

He's imparting that the human belief system is
flawed, even if creativity inspired. Closed-
mindedness is the enemy, especially when one has
access to all of the available *factual* knowledge
through the internet, and from history.

The good beasties representing positive
emotions such as love, empathy, and kindness,
choose to dance around Voice and Terra, who are at
the easels. Actually, seeing these beasties dancing
around onstage allows Voice and Terra the
opportunity to finally accept what they have always
believed. And their belief system indeed changed
upon understanding the reality of the situation as
Impulse projected it.

Terra and Voice now respond,

"Enlightened business of the claw reaches
out to touch, yet mauls,
The flesh, the soul, the bonds of cold,
demeaning self-control,
Distracted yet from the timely set, of
requirements of human debt,
Without the sense to feel remiss, I believe
there's something to this."

Terra and Voice know, through their own
atoms' pidis connected to Impulse, that we owe our
future to our past, and those who do not learn this do
not survive.

I again explain to them all the closed-minded and manufactured senses that cause pain,

> "A beastie is not just human, psychically
> diminished ruin,
> Devoured through and through in darkly
> depths within."
> Failed like a withered blowhard, delinquent
> emotional shit-hard,
> Lost in a ghastly brain fart, disgusted that
> it's so hard."

Yet again misunderstanding the words, the bad beasties believe that Voice means that they are the best of choices. They consider these lyrics to be compliments?

Here we stand, with bad beasties believing they are good, and good beasties not caring what the bad beasties believe because they feel they offer positive experiences for their humans. And that those pleasing internal chemicals and memories are all that are needed to provide reinforcement of their positive beliefs. A proverbial stand-off—between two sets of emotions for control of the situation—is taking place right in front of everyone.

Each of the musicians, also now aware due to Impulse's prompting, are flashing back to memories of childhood trauma—demeaning behavior by responsible adults, the bullies in school, mean bosses at work, people who have taken advantage of them throughout their lives. These memories are bringing each musician's bad beasties personas to life, and that causes the loss of control of their subconscious memory emotions.

Great, just great! This adds the anxiety beastie to the mixture, and the chemical concoction with the humans is becoming toxic.

Now, *all* of the beasties are dancing to the music (some of these beasties are the creators of the inspiration and skill sets of the musicians, which help them to understand how to play and perform).

At the onset of the conflict, Voice, in order to distract them, steps between the good and bad beasties and sings,

> "Whether we be strong or weak, whether there's a final peak,
> Clever, life is, so to speak; a vacuum of aloneness."

Impulse moves us to join Voice at center stage singing,

> "Grip the charcoal, control your grasp, paint by numbers without a task.
> Black and white oblivious lapse; the actions that define us."

It's our admirable attempt to turn anxiety into creativity, Impulse relates to me.

While the beasties dance around, I walk to the easel holding my meteor painting, and place a new posterboard on it. I draw a giant heart shape in red marker.

PunkHead begins the chant and everyone joins in, including the good and bad beasties, all happily proud of their contributions to their humans.

"Beasties! Beasties! Beasties! Beasties!
Beasties! Beasties! Beasties! Beasties!
Beasties! Beasties! Beasties! Beasties!"

Next, PunkHead blasts into a powerhouse appeal,

"Beasties live with hopes of chance; change their queer by circumstance.
No special needs or crucial greed, just find a place to be at ease.
No one understands their pain, superficial attempt to gain,
A freedom from their madness."

PunkHead's words are validation for the bad beasties, who quickly return to their humans, content that they are accepted as misunderstood and traumatized beings, certainly not evil ones.

And the good beasties, now with a better understanding of the other side, offer warm support to their humans. In some connotation, besides defeating irrational beliefs, this could be a story of lost causes and unexpected successes; *all* beasties deserve to be happy, even the bad ones—especially if they're only considered to be "bad" when judged so by others.

Impulse knows it isn't easy for humans to change ingrained programming so that other humans can recognize those changes in behavior. Impulse is sympathetic and helps to create happier beasties by educating their humans. But each person has unique qualities—their own thoughts and behaviors; free will; their own decisions to be a positive or negative member of a group, or to change their mind; and/or of experiencing their own emotions evoked when *facts* are presented. A human is, by all intents and purposes, a... definition... of... choice...

Impulse sings poetry through me to assure all of the humans that they can control their beasties, if they *choose* to do so,

> "Never worry that beasties exist.
> Within that space of time persists,
> A fluid reminder of the lost track of time;
> Were there any involving the mind, beyond what is normal?
> A beastie is formally challenged to be what it's formed."

The underlying desire—the need of each person; an important part of the human spirit—may be their drive to be unique (and this desire, ironically, is most always misunderstood by their fellow humans). We sing this, hoping to remove their madness of trying to be like someone, or everyone, else,

> "Unique is better than sameness;
> A freedom from their madness..."

Next, everyone joins me and, as we sing, Impulse releases the audience back to our reality in time, and vocally concludes the song with...

> "Unique is better than sameness."

Although the fans, while still, could feel only the heartbeat-drumbeat, they now react in real time with overwhelming approval and wild applause.

Terra approaches the easel where I last drew and draws a beautiful heart shape intertwined with mine.

Message received...

Chapter Eight
"Dinosaur Rock"

In pondering everything that's happened, I believe that this, in the here and now, may be the catalyst, the real movement, toward the success of Impulse's mission to find emotional and intellectual triggers to evolve the humans' behaviors, so that their beasties don't encourage the planet to destroy humanity.

I feel so lucky to be here, participating in this event!

Wait! What did I just say? Have I just learned that Impulse's mission is to save humanity from being destroyed by the planet? *We* are about to be destroyed—by the *planet*? (I guess being aware has its benefits and drawbacks).

Impulse just conveyed this message to everyone onstage; they now know, too. Voice steps back in to lead his show, *totally* aware that the message from Impulse is real to the entire band.

The wind gusts, and the posterboard with Terra's and my interlocking hearts flies off the easel. My drawing of a meteor streaking toward Terra's easel is now visible again. Could we be expecting a restart of earth's evolutionary experiment?

Impulse has conveyed to us the need to save our dying planet from abuse and neglect; the activities and beliefs of humans must evolve their emotional spirit as a species planet-wide, and humans must find a way to make other humans more aware. We who have little, yet precious, time to exist must—by changing the core subconscious belief system humans now harbor—take action so that we terminate the continuous erosion of the planet's surface. The challenge of our reality against this flight of fantasy is about to take shape; we'll see that this is a much bigger picture.

Just imagine that only an Impulse is driving this revelatory experience toward us.

When we look deep into Terra's eyes into her soul, past the memories, the fear, the experiences, we see a picture of a ravaged earth in the form of her heart. Her belief is that the planet will be completely devastated by humans, destroyed slowly beyond any previous comprehension.

In order to keep a destructive monster of sadness from releasing itself within her, Terra has externally surrounded herself with positive beasties. But she sees the sadness monster reflected in the words and actions of herself, and of society. Sometimes her friends, family members, and acquaintances are corrupted beyond communication by the negativity of others. From what I understand of her sentiments, she feels that misunderstood emotions, thinking, and reality, cause irrational behavior, *and* actions she can't always control. This makes her very sad.

I've never been allowed so deeply into the heart of another person, let alone one this pure. The only way I can describe it is to say that it's like being invited into the soul of where all good grows. Terra represents all the good of planet Earth that the universe wants to protect. To the depths of my being, I feel true love for this woman. If only I could ease her pain, calm her fears, be the one in her life to make her happy. She's the perfect mate, but any hormonal or wishful inclination to pursue that human dream is stifled by Impulse as we get back to work on the mission.

Like Terra, this sci-fi rock of a planet may very well believe that the cause of its misery is its own internal struggle on its own surface. Terra Firma avoids, or repels, the diseases it believes are irresponsible human behaviors, much like Terra herself does. Mother Nature has trouble with her beasties—these humans she has parasitically eating away at her atmosphere and landscape. Similar maladies… similar symptoms… similar results?

This gives me a surreal urge to add some levity to the situation, to relieve some stress and pressure. Voice's next song allows me to do just that. Via a volcano or geyser, the planet releases its internal pressure; humans also need a release, so they can establish balance between their internal expectations and disappointments.

Vibe flashes a hand cue to the band, and they kick into the heavy with oriental highlights satire rock and roll sound of "Dinosaur Rock," Voice's attempt to correlate the past with the present to protect the future.

Based on his favorite movie, *Godzilla*, this song relates man's direct destruction of the planet to the movie about a creature of man's making doing the same. Sure, everything has its *time* on the planet, and what happens during that time becomes *history*, so why not relate the time prior to the last planetary destruction to the current crisis? Meteor or meat-eater, what will it be that destroys humanity?

I can sense in our proximity the monster I saw in Terra's core, in her fearful eyes; the ultimate, narcissistically evil monster, larger than life, supported by the fear and anger of the populace.

Dick T.Raitor remains a symbol of destruction, just like Tyrannosaurus Rex represented sixty-eight million years ago, and just like Godzilla represented to a post-nuclear, fearful world. I feel an eerie chill. Impulse allows me into the minds of the audience, their thought processes and deep feelings, their visualizations of potential consequences. Being inside so many human minds, reading so many belief systems, encountering so many irrational beasties, is rocking me into an awareness I never, in my wildest dreams, imagined.

Wait a minute here… For explanation's sake, all of this mental analysis is happening within us in mere *seconds* of human time. I have to remind myself now that time keeps moving, even though my Impulse can stop or slow our reality… A lucky talent of his for me to experience! That said, we somehow still have enough universal strength to give Terra, Voice, and their throngs of followers the help they need to deal with a monster that can destroy the earth.

I have always believed that comedy can be a defense against irrational behavior, but would it be possible to use comedy to counter monsters like T.Raitor? Impulse begins by activating everyone's imagination within the parietal lobe of their brains. (It now appears like with any magic, that the ability to produce a mass hallucination is simple, when you know how the trick is done).

The thundering beat and crunching guitars evoke a unified movement in the audience; up and down, up and down, emulating the ponderous gaits of the prehistoric beasts that roamed the earth millions of earth years ago. Impulse projects a vision into this huge mass of minds. Now they see, in their minds, standing right in front of us all, a full-size prehistoric Tyrannosaurus Rex! Straight outta my fifth-grade science books, and my favorite Godzilla movies! Like an expedition to a lost world in some Jules Verne science fiction novel, here we are witnessing something unbelievable, previously unimaginable! The audience continues their up and down, up and down T. Rex trot!

Impulse moves me to the front of the stage to sing,

"He's a big Tyrannosaurus, about eighty feet long,
Big and ugly and awful strong.
Got a roar that rings like a gong,
Just leaving destruction as he moves along."

He's describing Dick T.Raitor as the extinct dinosaur.

Since my mind's linked to my Impulse pidi, I have full-on knowledge about Dick T.Raitor being the corporate and political tool of greed and corruption. It's a weird cosmic coincidence, this—appearing here at the Park during this concert, *and* my body being invaded by this amazing Impulse. I feel completely capable of doing what needs to be done. I'm unafraid and I have no anxiety. I accept this major download of universal knowledge.

Dick T.Raitor's despicable plan is an attempt for him, along with his cronies and allies, to become the controllers of all physical resources of Earth. Since they feel that they have enough support, influence, and funding to push that agenda. They were able to infiltrate and bribe the concert promoter, paid all the expenses of this concert, just to be able to appear to be aligned with Voice and his audience. Money talks, walks, sings, and dances in T.Raitor's world.

"DT," as he is known among his followers, believes that if the lie is good enough and told often enough, the innocent and ignorant will buy it. And that's all he needs to overthrow common sense and the rule of law.

Past history shows that such actions by this type of person have seriously and negatively affected humanity but, somehow, many people forgot and forget—they don't teach history to the next generation because they are either too naïve, or they don't want to remember because it suits them better not to. I'm not being judgmental, it's just a realization.

It appears to me that we may have gone from the utopian fantasy of a perfect earth to a potential apocalyptic end-of-the-planet, ripe for another meteor to crash into us and start us all over again (all this thought and analysis happens in mere nanoseconds of human reality time as Dick T.Raitor is beckoning his minions to the front of his platform).

We continue the song, singing,

> "Jenny Lou, playing on the steps doesn't know that he's loose yet;
> A big dinosaur from another age about to crush her porch in a rage.
> Run, Jenny Lou! He's coming after you!

He's got no sense of humor and he plans on eating you.
There's nothing you can do, there's nothing you can say;
Turn up the radio and hope he'll dance away."

The humans and their beasties dance to the music. Within a minute or so, they derive Voice's message from his lyrics, music, and humor about the hypocritical prehistoric relic who in climbing onto a small stage attempting to gain attention. Some of the citizens actually abandon their placards and dance to the infectious beat. This evokes around them less aggressive beasties, and the citizens' behavior is calmer.

As the familiar chorus ensues, DT appears on the riser and starts tossing handfuls of cash money toward the dancing crowd. He shouts into his microphone,

"Dinosaur!"

Everyone including his supporters respond,

"Dinosaur Rock!"

DT yells back,

"I'm making lots of money and I like it a lot."

Voice inserts himself into the song,

"He does the..."

And DT again shouts into his microphone,

"Dinosaur!"

DT's minions again shout,

"Dinosaur Rock."

Voice sings,

"It's the same old game;
It's the same old shlock."

Dick T.Raitor and his subordinate trolls are on his platform (as if it's *his* own rally) and, in his delusion, he considers Voice's fans *his own* followers, embracing *his* message! Thankfully, I can easily see that his supporters are the few gathered to the front of his riser. I'm relieved to see that the rest of the audience sings along in a demeaning manner *against* DT and his people.

Impulse informs me that there is, here and now, a lesson that must be taught. The power of this transcended being within me allows us (yes, Impulse and I are an "us" now) to employ a mental manipulation of the entire audience. Impulse taps into the mass' mindset and projects to them a common image.

He creates the illusion in everyone's mind that DT and his cronies look exactly like that giant, terrible lizard, T. Rex!—green as greed, with a mind the size of a peanut, plopped within the body of a giant eating machine. DT now looks as scary as his message.

The purpose of this message from Impulse is to teach the masses that, if humans do not unify to repel the monster, they will be consumed by it.

Voice and the band continue the song as DT flings handfuls of one-dollar bills to his citizens. They clamor to grab the flying moulah; it's repulsive to watch all that pushing and shoving to grab such minimal rewards.

Voice's next section is making fun of the state of the music business, where everything is rehashed to new generations, including the music he loves; his feeling that corporate control of the creative process has been destroying the music business.

Impulse and I sing his allegory,

> "There's always been a music that sounds like it.
> It's a heavy kind of dance and it goes like this:
> Put one foot forward and shake-a your hips,
> Then jump up and down 'til the record skips!"

To the band's delight, the humans shake their hips and jump about. Singing the next line, I lean into Terra all the while,

> "There's prehistoric passion in the rhythm of the drums,
> Hearts beating in the tarpits everybody's overcome."

I turn to Voice and the crowd and sing this warning,

> "You thought they were extinct, then you were surely fooled.
> Even though their brains are small, they really had a groove."

Together, Voice and I conclude the second verse, the lyrics of which humorously tell the listeners how to find the truth amidst the clatter of corporate messaging, since all media is owned by the offending parties,

> "So listen on your radio, tune in on your video—
> Really big sound from the days gone by.
> There's nothing you can do. There's nothing you can say.
> Turn up the radio and hope he'll dance away to the…"

Of course, DT doesn't believe that the joke is on *him*; he doesn't realize that the audience sees him as a monster! Again, he bellows into his microphone,

> "Dinosaur!"

Now, only his few devoted deviants respond,

> "Dinosaur rock!"

DT throws more money to his suck-ups and sings,

"I'm making lots of money and I like it a lot."

Voice rolls his eyes, and snidely slips in,

"He does the…"

"Dinosaur!"

DT yells, accidentally, on cue. His lackeys again bellow,

"Dinosaur rock!"

Voice concludes the statement,

"It's the same old game;
It's the same old shlock."

Several times, DT shouts,

"Dinosaur!"

Yet, now, each shout is followed by the *entire* audience echoing,

"Dinosaur rock!"

There's an accusatory tone in their voices. DT, ever narcissistic, believes that he's enraptured the crowd; he smiles and waves like he's won them over.

Impulse and I can tell that the crowd is loving their mass hallucination! Voice leads them in their favorite dance routine (easy steps they do at every show), and Vibe and the band solidify the beat. This time, they're mocking the monster, too! Everyone continues to jump up and down, clapping their hands to the beat and creating a thunderous echo of a dinosaur's feet shaking the earth. The joy created by the music unifies this mentally aligned mass—they're enjoying the visual anomaly and the adrenaline rush and the aural incursion! It's exhilarating for me to be part of this, too.

Several of the citizens and their corresponding beasties dance with new friends! They've seen the vision and decide that DT is not the person they were led to believe he is. They toss away their placards and their loyalty. The band's music is doing its powerful, positive job!

Vibe rips the audience into a frenzy with his next guitar solo, as the band backs him with churning chords blazing into the song's conclusion.

Voice's fans have had enough of the other duly-devoted-to-DT citizens. The fans' beasties react against the imposing citizens' beasties by ignoring them—the *worst* fate for an attention-demanding, narcissistic beastie, *and* their humans.

DT sees the crowd abandoning his ploy, even after throwing money to them. He and his suck-ups quietly back away from what may turn into a confrontation spurred by the raucous rock and roll. Some of his supporters' beasties are amending their actions; I can sense some of their humans changing their minds and beliefs about DT!

Some of the citizens' posters have blown onto the stage. Terra picks them up and puts all but two in a recycling bin offstage; she won't abide by any garbage, we know. She flips the two placards over; they're unmarked, so she places them on the easels.

Terra quickly and effortlessly draws the familiar shape of Planet Earth.

The music continues to throb and the audience pulses. Suddenly, all that can be heard is the drumbeat.

Impulse pushes us to dance our way to Terra, and to write one word on each poster:

"Stand" on one,

"Up" on the other.

I think to myself that, as the earthly saying goes, the proverbial tide appears to be turning.

Here and now, the prehistoric drumbeat becomes a marching, rallying beat...

Chapter Nine
"Stand Up and Be Counted"

Terra has made a sincere commitment to herself that she can, with her will and her hands, keep the environment from being more inundated with trash, thereby creating and re-instilling the beauty that the universe appreciates. (I only know this information because my Impulse has tapped deeply into her essence and shared this with me). It would be so easy to fall in love with her for all that she represents. She has no expectation of critical acclaim, profits, or any other such form of success from her art; she's just content that she's done it to the best of her ability. She creates art because she believes that she's innately driven to do so.

Sid continues the drum and bugle corps rhythm that sounds familiar to everyone; a parade march to inspire people. The impressive sound of an entire brass section and powerful drummers emanates from the stage, as the audience cheers and nods in approval. All those heads bouncing in unison is sheer joy to behold!

After having listened to this new album and having been a fan of Voice's work for years, I'm not surprised at all by the unification that motivates the audience. This group of musicians, gathered by their individual callings, ideals, and heartfelt beliefs, aggregate now to expend a joyous vibration, *and* important message.

I'm also not shocked by the diffusion of fact and fiction—a coping mechanism, really—in the minds of many of the hapless humans, especially the citizens, and their irrationally-influenced beasties.

They are moving in a blob, trying to reassess the situation, coddling themselves and their leader, Dick T.Raitor, over to the side of his riser. The music, though, really appeals to their basic patriotic instincts, just like John Philip Sousa marches in an Ohio State University half-time show. The music's universality resonates within them. It's the nostalgic music of Friday Night Football, and many of the citizens are torn between enjoying this sound or concentrating on their taskmaster's needs.

Many of the citizens, having accepted this music, mindlessly tap their feet to it. Their beasties are curious and join in, floating to the front of the stage. I'm witnessing not only a sea of humanity, but also their beasties exuding their panoply of human emotions!

Voice begins to sing to his allied masses in a key that attracts the full attention of the citizens, and dissipates their anger and divisiveness. Voice sings,

> "There's a call to arms in the world today.
> Fear and greed seem to lead the way,
> Driven by invertebrates who can't stand up,
> We've become their slaves."

Bringing in the universal vision that somehow Voice scripted, I chime in on the next line, singing,

> "To control your world and drive you mad,
> Make you think that it all has gone bad,
> Without a knowledge of the past,
> Or sense of logic, even if crass."

Terra and Voice reply,

"We'll take a pass!
Stand up and be counted!"

I sing,

"Listen! Heed the call!"

Terra and Voice chant,

"Stand up and be counted!"

I sing to Terra (with Voice's nod of approval),

"You're an individual."

Then, the three of us proudly exclaim,

"Stand up and be counted!"

Dick T.Raitor's ominous voice booms through the PA system. He challenges the band, and their message, grunting,

"Hey, you! Up against the wall!"

Voice and Terra counter with,

"Stand up and be counted!"

Dick T.Raitor interrupts with,

"You're no individual!"

Miraculously, Impulse and I—WE—see that Voice is emotionally uniting the crowd and their beasties together even more! The disparity among these beings is dissipating, along with their contradicting agendas, beliefs, opinions, facts, behaviors, and reactions! They are beginning to realize that they have a common enemy in *anyone* who would divide them for the sake of profits, especially at the risk of destroying the planet.

The Sousa-like march continues as the brass section pumps along, which gives the roadies the opportunity to locate and unplug Dick T.Raitor's hijack of the sound system. DT's trolls attempt sneaky and distracting paths around the roadies, creating a macabre dance of wires and cables.

I can't resist. With a little mental manipulation, I'm able to telepathically convey to everyone (except the hard-core DT dependents suckling the financial teat of their overlord) that their elected official has determined that they're not smart enough to make their own decisions. This causes their beasties to be agitated.

Voice challenges his fans again,

"Who among us will heed the call."

Terra adds,

"Support the cause to freedom's hall?"

Voice sings to Terra,

"With a sincere sense of it all."

And she replies to him,

> "As we stand up, see the cracks in their
> wall."

Voice points to the side of the stage where DT
and his minions have settled, and sings,

> "To control our food, our air and minds,
> Truth so painful, sheep stay blind."

Terra responds,

> "Destroying our climate is so unkind.
> There is no sense in letting it slide.
> IF THIS IS THE FUTURE,
> WE'VE RUN OUT OF TIME!"

Terra and Voice repeat the chorus to the crowd,
many of whom are mouthing the words!

> "Stand up and be counted!"

As I point to DT, I sing,

> "Watch the bullies fall!"

And from the speakers, again, comes,

> "Stand up and be counted!"

I reiterate my point,

> "Many individuals."

Everyone sings in unison,

"Stand up and be counted!"

This is countered again by the irritating timbre of Dick T.Raitor's voice, threatening,

"Hey, you! Up against the wall!"

An overwhelming vocal attack is emitted from the stage, with the help of the audience,

"STAND UP AND BE COUNTED!"

T.Raitor pummels the audience with his demeaning defense, proclaiming to all once more,

"You're no individual!"

Since Terra's goal to save the environment is aligned with Voice's goal to change the political structure to the benefit of all (not just the wealthy), we, but really just Impulse, employ some universal magic by planting into the humans' minds pictures of the current climate destruction causing Terra Firma to use its own "antibodies"—the weather—to remove irritants that cause its illness. And by irritants, I mean *human* irritants (Earth tries to scratch the itch in its own way).

Hurricanes, earthquakes, drought, fire, floods, and eruptions are messages to us from within the planet's soul. There's a subconscious thought process that allows a self-sustaining, living organism, evolved over billions of years, to survive, while isolated from contact with other celestial sources.

Yes, humans may be like "blood cells" to a planet, but even human blood can contain a cancerous, diseased cell, infecting a planetary "body." Scientifically speaking, in human physiology, a diseased cell in the human body is attacked by evolved proteins produced by plasma cells in the blood to neutralize potentially toxic bacteria and pathogens. By recognizing a unique molecule causing the malady, the healthy molecules can help the ill one, and change it. Our approach may have the ability to trigger the call from within the humans to set that change in motion!

The ability of any antibody to communicate with the other components of a human's immune system, through its fragment-crystallizable region located at the base of the Y chromosomes in human DNA, may be translatable. By me! Okay, *us*. On a massive scale!

So, in order to trigger the earth's antibodies to ease up on destroying the irritants—humans—we must work on changing the human's irrational thoughts and beliefs! Maybe this can be done to humans if we look at them as scientifically similar. Voice, Terra, music, art, and positive thinking may be the collective antibody able to defend Terra Firma from the growing disease spread by Dick T.Raitor and his ilk.

The band changes the entire mood of the song, from the up-tempo proclamation of unity and courage to a somber funeral dirge similar to a march played for caskets returning from a war (the sound attributed to a feeling of despair and sadness). The mood and the spirit of the beasties are immediately affected by this musical shift.

The essence of pain is reflected in Voice's ominous chants of poetic warning,

> "They attack our culture, attach our bonds,
> Detach our future, they'd rather build bombs.
> They divide to conquer,
> And take our funds."

The band continues to churn the style of music that causes perplexion, anxiety and concern, to which Voice continues his call to action,

> "We can take down their egos, open their flaws,
> Teach them some lessons about passing bad laws."

Voice shouts to the audience,

> "Stand up to the bullies! Stand up to the fear!
> Stand up to the cowards! Stand up to the sheep.
> We'll stand up as humans, stand for our needs."

Voice hammers his message vociferously to his fellow denizens on this spinning rock known as Earth. They make it clear to the masses that this may be their last chance to defend their way of living against the monsters that could destroy the planet itself.

At this point I'm considering all of the power of Impulse and I combined, but now as a singular action. Being more comfortable using *my* newfound mass hallucination-inducing, mind-manipulation skills on some of these lesser-evolved brains (especially after having shown the masses, via their minds' eyes, a future vision of a climate destroyed by human recklessness), I opt to start the next verse singing a truth which all must understand,

> "Bullies come and bullies go;
> History has the skill to show."

Voice adds,

> "What happened before, we now know,
> Can happen today, if we don't grow."

I sing to the crowd of history, hoping they get the message,

> "Small-minded beings inhabit the earth;
> Millions of creatures, primordial birth—
> Beings not capable of filling the dearth,
> Breeding new bullies without any worth."

Voice asks,

> "Can we defeat them?
> They seem so immersed."

It felt really good to lay that on the humans! Chemicals in Impulse's and my—our!—body are causing a tingling sensation... Our epidermis is reacting with small bumps along our arms... I believe the crowd may have this sensation, too!

Terra and Voice, like an aural stimulant, point their fingers at the audience and thunder,

"STAND UP AND BE COUNTED!"

I point at the citizens, who are now really enjoying the rousing marching music, and I challenge them,

"Hey, you! Hear the call."

Terra and Voice repeat their defiant jubilation,

"STAND UP AND BE COUNTED!"

I look to Terra, as I sing confirmation of her personal commitment,

"If you're an individual…"

She smiles at me and nods! The entire crowd responds with a massive callback,

"STAND UP AND BE COUNTED!"

I sing, pointing directly towards Dick T.Raitor and his obsequious cronies,

"Hey, you! Watch the bullies fall!"

The crowd again responds,

"STAND UP AND BE COUNTED!"

And I chant this reminder of strength to the weak-minded,

"Sheep need not stall!"

The crowd joins Voice, Terra, and the band at full-on stadium-style volume, singing,

"STAND UP AND BE COUNTED!"

And I add, my arms fanning outward to embrace them all,

"We're all *individuals*…"

Then, roaring from the crowd comes,

"STAND UP AND BE COUNTED!"

I respond, this time pointing to the punks and protestors defying Dick T.Raitor,

"HEY YOU! Time to move that wall!"

The entire mob of glorious humans rises up to exclaim,

"STAND UP AND BE COUNTED!"

And as the unified mass of emotions, humans and beasties alike, good, bad and indifferent, happy and sad, singing in unison to the outer realms of the universe, choose to point out the obvious:

"You're ALL individuals!"

We made progress. I can feel it! I can see it! All of the humans, including the *citizens*, stood up and sang out!

In the garden of nature, surrounded by the trappings of society, among the vast variety of plants, animals and humans gathered... The cosmic, healing rays of sunlight, mixed with the humans' chemically created, shared reactions... Thoughtful influence and stirring music... Like the first days of homo erectus, evolution may have manifested change—right there in front of me.

As we wrap up the song like on the record, everyone in unison, onstage and off, with purpose and conviction, recite the message that everyone now understands:

"STAND UP!"

Chapter Ten
"Empathy"

To the vociferous cheers of an audience that may be 30,000 strong at this point, Voice and the band announce to the audience that it's intermission, thank them for their adulation, and wind their ways towards the backstage area. Voice would seriously like to know why Dick T.Raitor has been allowed to cut into the show and heads off to find his manager and the concert promoter.

That monster who crashed this party has disappeared into a heavily guarded, out-of- the-way motorhome, and the few trolls that continue to support him have scampered off to spread their vile hate to align others still loyal to their cause. Many of the formerly-completely-seduced-righteous citizens' inner beasties have completely changed, and I can see many of them emulating the lessons imparted in the first half of the concert!

Which gives us some time to analyze everything that's happened up to this point. By continuing to refer to the proverbial "us" I refer to my Impulse and I. Having been extremely cooperative throughout this "process" of co-mingling our beings, I convey that *we* are hungry and thirsty; we need sustenance. I down a couple of swigs of water and a few bites of some snacks, and gaze upon the scene with wide-eyed wonder. Impulse is intrigued by the sensation of water running into our system and the process of food being digested, but there are more important things.

The stage is empty and interstitial instrumental music is heard from the PA system. No one notices as I sit cross-legged at my security guard position down stage right of the stage gathering my thoughts, allowing Impulse to focus on his mission. The path is now clear, but some more mental magic may be needed to get the desired necessary result. We are on our way. That I can sense.

Universal knowledge and advanced technology allow us to project in front of us hologram-like charts and graphs, analyses of actions, calculations, interstellar movements aligned, chemical changes and reactions, which assist us, via mathematical equations predicting percentages of success, in deducing outcomes.

Our projections could also be seen by Terra as she gazes from afar, not sure whether she should interrupt, but instead chooses to follow Voice backstage. Other transcended souls within the audience members have gravitated toward the stage, many of whom can also see the projections.

It's interesting to notice the variety of informed beings here in this crowd, on this day, in this location—an aggregation of positive, life-giving auras, who can create a catalytic force of change! I feel the presence of good and bad humans who are able to see, experience, and *control* beasties around them. But I also still have a strange sense of an evil transcension in our midst.

I could clearly see Terra's beasties, especially the one she refers to internally as "Empathy." Empathy beasties evolve kindness beasties and kindness is the currency of the universe. Narcissistic humans regress that evolution.

This seems a simple enough principle, except that the basic conundrum, from birth to death, deep down for every human is how do we become one type of person or another?

Since we cannot *force* change on others without *damage*, including to a planet, can we *influence* change without damage? And save the planet?

We tap into the entire cosmic consciousness of the audience, the planet, and all the beams of light reaching Earth on this beautiful day in paradise. Doing so will yield a better outcome in our scientific analysis, a more desirable end than only a temporary charge to human brain chemicals leading to anticipation or anxiety.

The ominous concrete towers looming in the distance surrounding this idyllic nature preserve gave me the presence of mind to check out the Earth's electronic communications for more clues.

Since all radio, television and internet communication is wireless, and the signals are nothing but waves and particles of matter (just like Impulse), access to all knowledge, opinions, facts, and fallacies, are readily available for our research. Through mere concentration, we can garner the needed knowledge and project it via three-dimensional holograms, then compare, contrast, and confirm a myriad of data about the humans' destruction of their homes.

Reality, as portrayed by the "news" channels, messengers, and reporters on the televised waves, is consistently divisive, pitting tribes of humans against each other, mostly for power or control, and usually causing many souls internal and external damage by the few who choose to take advantage. These messages about the actions of the evil are interspersed with vapid advertisements, attempting to sell people on frivolous products and distracting experiences. Impulse queries of me asking if this is all human life is supposed to be about.

I notice that all purveyors of ill have *justification* for their actions, reinforced by the talking head conveying the information, *and* the evil collaborators can easily justify blaming any problems on others. It's pointed out to me even further when we notice that evil humans are often wealthy and suffer very few repercussions for the results of their ill-intended actions.

Some claim a religious entity given right to power, alluding to the *fact* that an ominous deity exists to *save* them, that they are "anointed" by said being to be the conduit to others, to speak to and convey upon weak-of-mind humans the will, spirit and knowledge of their *Gods*. These people are surrounded by the *most* despicable of the beasties, greed, hate, apathy and fear, and are seen cowering from reality right before them. They may know, but do not choose to relay to their followers, that the planet Earth itself is the *heaven* promised by the snake-oil salesmen of religion.

Sure, there are many who seek *hope* and, for a totally irrational reason, may also have *faith* in a non-factual, non-deliverable, imaginary promise. But the greedy beings who manipulate the poor and unsure with promises of salvation in an *afterlife* rob these beings from their opportunity to transcend to being a better human while they are here in *this* life. Organized religion, supported by unbridled financial rewards, corrupts the manipulators, who impart intense fear upon those who are easily brainwashed;

and the manipulators, to sustain their power, target the youngest humans for culture breeding. This falsely-justified mental child abuse—the inciting of children to blindly believe non-facts—is very likely where all human suffering begins.

My inundation of data absorbed into our system via our worldwide scan, and download to my subconscious pidi, causes my mind to expand, and although my heart is actually beating calmly, I completely understand the complexity of our task. We contemplate our next foray into bringing about positive change via music, art, and knowledge. If given the chance, the human mind can expand, similar to the universe's ability to also continually do so.

The intermission music allows us to enter a deep meditative state of awareness. In order to avoid a disturbance in our meditation, we slow time, *and* the movements of Terra, Voice, and the band, as they make their way to the stage to start the second half of the show. The audience, we can feel, is ready for more entertainment.

In these frozen moments as earth time delays, Impulse sings quietly to internal self as if speaking to otherworldly beings:

> *I took a few deep breaths; took my mind off*
> *the mess; into the outer reaches of the*
> *cosmos I leapt,*
> *Where questions were not asked, because no*
> *one there is tasked, with beings with brains*
> *evolving.*
> *They keep needing to know how and why, if*
> *my quest has found a light to shine.*

At this moment, he is able to attach the subconscious minds of Voice and Terra in their currently slowed state of action and bring them with us for a journey to reach what could be the pinnacle of their open minds' imagination.

In a blink of an eye, we are all now far away from the planet (this is absolutely my first experience outside of a human body, but I sense that Terra and Voice have experienced this before). All minds are attached to Impulse's pidi, and we appear to travel at light speed to a different visual perspective. We slow just as quickly, and the immenseness of the universe is apparent to all.

Impulse sings through me,

> *There was a calm in the universe, as the experience fell exclusively to the human experiments, affecting no one, and nothing, in the outer worlds. Yet essential in evolving the universal goals.*
> *I felt the calm, it was strengthening. I knew my fate and my destiny. I felt the resolve to accomplish my mission to understand the cause of those irrational emotions...*

In a split second of human time, we appear to be whisked upon a beam of light to Earth's Moon, a barren orbiting rock (a familiar view of Terra Firma, having seen photographic and video likenesses from this distance). This image of scientific reality carries with it a history of wonder, followed by scientific proof of truths and facts—all developed by ever-evolving intelligent human beings.

Even when presented with scientific evidence and universal knowledge, I do still have some strange doubt deep in my subconscious, developed, I can tell, by my own childhood trauma, bad personal relationships, and incorrect information acquired from unreliable sources.

Impulse queries me, and humankind,

> *Here, I see the difference, but fail to see*
> *how, one can choose to be one or the other;*
> *Is it math or science, father or mother?*

Impulse notices that I am not only picturing my childhood in our combined mind (which he explains elicits emotion-engaging chemicals within my body), but I'm also evoking my curiosity about people like Dick T.Raitor, his trolls, and the humans who choose to endorse that negative behavior.

Impulse tries to break it down for me, confirming the explanation using knowledge sent from his pidi directly into my mentally challenging subconscious belief system to question, at their source, all my illogical motifs.

With continued thought of Dick T.Raitor, we sing,

> *What beastie are you, and what are you*
> *made of, controlled from within and unable*
> *to feel love?*
> *Does nature, genetics, society, universal*
> *guidance, or a combination of these,*
> *attributes, deflections, unguided sad*
> *reflections, cause one human to be kind and*
> *fair?*

Of course, the answer is obvious to the thinking beings but, in this momentary pause, we consider the *opposite* of the beasties "kind" and "fair"—an evil, presenting itself as capable of destroying most of the evolved human life on the planet (and who have blatantly, and uninvited, presented themselves at this celebratory event). We reflect upon the sentiment Dick T.Raitor presents, who is:

> *Another obsessed with power will just not care.*

In the time of a human eye-blink, we return to the stage.

Voice and the band plugged in, poised, posed like statues, with Terra at her easels, are about to begin the second half of the show. The audience has begun to roar, cheer, and clap, sensing the beginning of the second half as I slowly rise to begin my *job*.

Voice and the band begin the first song in this set, a traditionally mid-twentieth century popular rock and roll musical style sometimes referred to as doo-wop—one that will hopefully help influence open minds to tame beasties.

Voice mans the front of the stage. Behind him are four back-up vocalists, *Birdy and The Tweets* (the lead singer sports a pompadour wig, resembling Conrad Birdie's from the musical "Bye Bye Birdie"—the ultimate film about music-for-profit).

The band barrels into the upbeat rhythm, their voices packing the speakers with that incredible wall of sound. The fans are happy as clams to have the concert rockin' again! All attention is on the stage as

Voice leads the performers with his words of wisdom (disguised as frivolous fun),

> "The beastie, Empathy, can shake your core;
> Makes you feel deeply what you never felt before.
> If you have the conscience to help one another,
> Empathy is Mother Nature's lover."

The audience and their beasties are loving this!

In the blink of a human eye and to everyone's surprise, including my own, Birdy pushes Voice out of the way and takes over, singing the lead, and modifying Voice's lyrics! Voice demurs and goes sidestage to Terra and her easels. Birdy sings emphatically, akin to a smarmy salesman trying to sell what people don't want or need,

> "The beastie, Fear, can shake your core;
> Makes you feel deeply what you never felt before.
> Creates no conscience to help one another.
> Fear is not Mother Nature's lover."

Perverting Voice's original lyrics even more, Birdy continues his poisonous snake oil salesman pitch,

> "The beastie, Greed, can shake your core;
> Makes you feel deeply what you never felt before.
> Destroys the conscience to help another.
> Greed is definitely not nature's lover."

The backup singers, as if this is all a joke, slovenly and facetiously drawl,

"Nature's loverrrrrrrrr…"

Voice and Terra look at me, calmly gesturing about this insurrection that is taking place, *and* if I was able to do something about it!

We all look on as Birdy rips off his fake pompadour hairdo revealing Dick T.Raitor hiding beneath! He grabs a saxophone and honks out a catchy squonking ditty. The audience laughs, enamored with the show and unaware that any of this is an effrontery. The Tweets employ elegant choreography in order to block the roadies and the band from regaining control of the show. Across the stage struts the self-appointed Mr. Saxophone, as his Tweets glide and shuffle to the beat!

Dick T.Raitor ends his squawky sax solo, and moves to the microphone, supported by the Tweets' doo-wops,

"The beastie, Hate, can shake your core!
Makes you feel deeply what you never felt before!
Manipulates the conscience; to hell with one another!
Hate cannot be mother nature's lover."

Security and roadies attempt to remove a scowling Dick T.Raitor, who, in a hope to buy leniency, suddenly tosses handfuls of dollar bills at the staff, the band, and the audience. As if that wasn't presumptuous enough, imparting his classic arrogant and narcissistic élan, Dick T.Raitor takes a bow as though he alone has triumphed here! Then, coward that he is, he skedaddles offstage to flee any repercussions.

Voice, Terra, and I can see the results of Dick T.Raitor's presence. The audience is completely surrounded by the negative beasties evoked by Dick T.Raitor's call to action. Is this the moment when the negativity within every single fan wins, and the masses decide to support Dick T.Raitor in his conquest of wills?

What we, the trio in the know, can sense is that the fear beasties and the hate beasties are posing a question: If, by removing their *own* fears and hatred—instilled in them in early childhood, and secured by their subconscious irrational belief systems—can they no longer *be* feared or hated? Simultaneously, the greed beasties are questioning their need for all things which are unnecessary.

In the here and now onstage, all attention is on me (I'm trying to reach the intellect, the spirit, the unknown element of stardust that makes humans unique in the universe). I take the mic in my hand. Yes, life exists everywhere, but only on earth does any creature sing, as I do now,

> "The beastie, HOPE, will shake your core.
> Makes you feel deeply what you never felt before;
> Enlarges your conscience to help one another.
> Hope is truly mother nature's lover."

Voice and Terra join me, and Vibe and the band ... all of us vocally bring this lesson in humankind to a resounding and uplifting conclusion—the spirited music, the soul-elevating backup voices proclaiming,

"Empathy!"

As Terra, referring to our Earth's woes, responds with,

"You see it in the floods and in the fires..."

And I add,

"You see it in the hurricanes of human desire..."

We all sing again, this time in multiple harmonies,

"Empathy!"

Terra's angelic voice then proclaims,

"You feel it in the panic to your cries..."

Voice answers, his voice atop the clouds,

"Your actions show your feelings."

Terra and I join in,

"As your spirit starts to rise..."

The audience knows this song, this word! They join in—a gargantuan, unified chorale of understanding,

"EMPATHY..."

And Voice, Terra, and I joyfully jump in,

"...Drives you like an engine, deep inside,
To do what's right, no matter there's no prize!"

We all proclaim, defiantly! This final choral escalation of voices concludes the song! It's as if the entire audience, including their good and bad beasties, have experienced an epiphany, a climax of maximum magnitude...

"EMPATHY...
EMPATHY
STARTS
TO
RISE..."

Chapter Eleven
"Love and Let Love"

The audience's voices and applause resound, high atop the skyscrapers surrounding the Park. People a full mile away can hear, and feel, the tremendous surge of emotions generated by the humans and beasties here! The squirrels in the area don't even notice, and continue to forage for snacks, and the birds busily go about their unobtrusive daily activities of survival. Nature endures...

Terra, having bonded so completely, allows me to delve more deeply into her soul, which I can do by merely gazing into her eyes. I learn so much so quickly! I'm amazed, yet grateful, that an alien and a human can share so much, and nonverbally. If this is real—if I'm not trippin' and imagining it—it is truly special.

I sense in Terra a state of disbelief that this many people have shown up for this concert, *and* that evil has infiltrated this atmosphere, much like pollution on Earth. Though, since she and Voice can now clearly see and understand the beasties that plague the environment, she feels hopeful. And even though she has her own protective beasties and friends nearby, I can sense that she has some anxiety related to today's event. She believes that if she, with pride in her accomplishment, continues to produce her art and sing from her heart, she'll be able to educate, and communicate with others.

Terra is—for her propensity for balance, and fearlessness in the face of reality—one person everyone who knows her greatly respects. She spends much of her reality time reading, writing, singing and quietly solving problems related to what she feels are the crises of her personal universe, *and* she shares that awareness via art, song, and story. Among her friends, she has a reputation as a guru, one who always relays, from her full heart, her personal wisdom about life, love, and happiness.

Now, here, content with our unusual *relationship*, and her own deepest understanding of her current place in the real universe of existence, Terra doesn't hold back in finally unleashing her wry wit. I see her previously shrouded common-sensical and humorous outlook, her rationale. And I feel that her acuity could break bad against the face of evil!

As we all stand in front of the cheering audience, Terra picks up another discarded poster board, places it on the easel over my drawing of the meteor, and writes the word "LITTER" in black marker. She adds over the word the human symbol for "NO"... a big red circle with a line diagonally through it.

Until now, only Voice, Terra and the band members know that I am not part of the show, and that neither was Dick T.Raitor and his cronies. Voice cues the band and they begin the next song, a spiritual number featuring Terra singing. She places her new poster on the easel next to the artwork of the planet Earth.

As the band imparts an orchestral-like swell, the audience quiets and nestles in for the song. Terra addresses me, and explains her perspectives on the human condition, singing,

"Some say to live and let live is being alive,

They move about the planet, just trying to
survive,
Content as a bee provides for the hive,
As the queen, so serene, waits patiently to
die."

Terra singing Voice's lyrics, referencing
humans' short time on Earth, and achieving balance
and hope, continues,

"Some say that life is to experience the ride,
That feeling of being takes you to the ends
of time.
Why bother to be worried when a sickness
seeps inside?
Try to be one who can feel the sun, and lets
their lovelight shine."

To Terra, I respond telepathically, with
awkward humor:
*The evolution of the human genetic
experiment... The decisions humans make to affect
it... Humans have become lazy in their evolution,
negatively affected by their apathy, comfort, and
egocentric society... They have lost their will...*
The audience hears from me, though, Voice's
jaunty lyric,

"Without the drive to see outside,
Their driven genetic complacency..."

Voice then chimes in with his own words
highlighting his viewpoint of current society,

"Humans divided by decency believe in
impossibilities;
Enjoy the abundant delicacies; can't control
what is destiny."

As we sing, Terra, Voice, and I dance about onstage, much to the audience's amusement. All three of us look to the audience singing gloriously to…

"Just love and let love!"

There is no other beastie that can assist change better than the beastie, Love—the attribute of *all* forms of human love.

I am learning, from deep within Terra's mind, that the many facets of love are defined in so many connotations that humans can often be confused about an intended and actual meaning of the word. And Love beasties accompany everyone, which doesn't make it any easier, as meanings can include romantic or sexual love, familial love, maternal or paternal love, platonic love, friendship love, respect love, and simple affection for a person or object, or an imagined deity. And I can't fail to mention the all-too-often irrational beasties of "love" in the form of Possessiveness—used to deflect reality, control, or impose will upon others.

Terra sings again, oh, so poignantly,

"Some say that life is just a fantasy.
This hologram is not a true symbol of
reality.

3-D and so deep beyond the mind's
capacity;
We have become a victim of technology.

"Some say that life is just a history.
You try to make something that remains
your legacy;
Could be cast as revisionist memories.
To be whole inside, and feel the ride to
lovelight is free."

I feel like she's singing to me alone. Voice, standing right next to me, believes the same about himself, as does the entire audience. She has that ability.

In deep pidi research, I find that humans are sometimes detached from the desire to care for others. The reality of the path of human history—from early evolutionary awareness of mammals into manhood, through torturous periods caused by organized religion such as the Dark Ages, to an art-and-literature explosion called the Enlightenment Period, through an Industrial Revolution and a worldwide land grab to a modern era Technology Age—has been *rewritten* by electronic news to show history that pleases the powerful.

The music swirls as we lead the audience in a waltz-like romp, everyone is smiling and dancing.

Terra is singing of knowledge she couldn't possibly know, yet it's right there inside her as she sings Voice's lyrics. I join her in singing the final verse of this song,

"Some say that time and space are ju.
distractions.
Those who haven't lived them just cann.
fathom."

With but a wave of my hand, I stop time anc
everyone's movement for a brief moment and sing,

"I see the universe expanding toward the
horizon…"

And Terra joins me as we sing,

"We see the Earth … Another birth, could
be another victim."

Voice's message was about any child being
born to an irrational human, controlled by bad
beasties, who suffers and may struggle to survive,
just as each baby born to insect, animal, or plant
must. But humans are supposed to be evolving!
Terra continues the story,

"Some say we have a fate beyond our
means,
To be part of something larger as we live out
our dreams."

Again, with a wave of my hand, I catch
everyone's attention for a brief moment to share my
own unique perspective, emotionally singing,

"Scattered among all human screams."

Terra sings directly to the thousands of people in front of us,

"Try to be defining!"

To which I add, emphatically,

"Always be shining!"

And she answers with,

"Your lovelight gleams."

A *lovelight* appearing in the cosmos is generated by the energy of trillions of good beasties existing on planet earth in every form of bacteria, plankton, single cell beings, and the gamut of evolving species!

That special wholesome radiation generated by positivity affects all things in the giant body of the Universe, much like adrenaline and other chemicals do within humans' bodies. The lovelight is a spirit that can be quantified, directed, amplified, and generated by the will of the beings, and the choice that the being makes to let their lovelight shine indeed affects all.

My personal lovelight is now gleaming, and I believe that everyone can see it beaming like a bright colorful light emitting from my chest where my heart exists! Eternal, unlimited energy is the reward of higher evolutionary growth, and control of that energy is a responsibility (because being a source of energy can make each human a volatile mass of chemicals).

Terra evolved before I did, and intersects me at *this* place at *this* time. She psychically conveys that a key to saving humanity may still exist on this planet, and she needs my help.

Voice and I, and what appears to be all of our beasties, singing with elevated humor, repeat the chorus,

> "Without the drive to see outside,
> Their driven genetic complacency,
> Humans, divided by decency,
> Believe in impossibilities,
> Enjoy the abundant delicacies,
> Can't control what is destiny."

Terra joins us all, singing,

> "Just love and let love!"

Now that I have a better understanding of the complex human emotions attached to the word "love," my Impulse allows me to feel the chemical reaction within us to, as they say, "fall in love" with Terra, the woman. This may compromise his mission providing me with a false belief that being in love with Terra would safely satisfy my human desire, satisfy his mission, or support the cause. Impulse doesn't choose to allow me to selfishly enjoy these moments of bliss, and we zone deep into ourselves, attempting to change our chemical balance to avoid embarrassment, or sadness, when reality sets in.

The audience responds to the song's conclusion with a joyous round of applause. We can see the good beasties celebrating the message and the music!

Now, I believe that I *know* Terra, but we may be having a human chemical concoction crisis!

Time to check the pidi…

Chapter Twelve
"Dive"

With a simple blink (I sense I'm getting good at this), we have slowed human earth time to a mere fraction of the humans' ability to interpret. All of their minds are deeply consumed with their own inner worlds; Terra, Voice, Vibe, the band members, the citizens, the trolls, the punks, the audience—all having something else on their minds, triggered by the words, music and environment. A clutter of drama, expectation, disappointment, anticipation, calendars, responsibilities, survival and propagation, all compete against the minimal moments of joy in an all-too-short existence when the time that is invented moves too fast.

That rare elusive elation which Voice and the band give the attendees, garners a response which is equally reciprocated to the performers; a mutual exchange of kindness and appreciation, if only for a moment or three. Right now, though, the humans don't need to live in the familiar concept of *time*—everyone is in a mental state they'd all like to attain, always.

With time stopped, I look at Voice. His eyes are smiling at Terra's, and hers are beaming back to him. They have a special bond. And the lyrics to all of his songs are eerily well-versed about the subjects with which Terra's most concerned, *and* our newly combined mission! I need to understand this interesting human anomaly better. With movement completely stopped around me, I walk over to them and stand between them, and proceed to stare into

Voice's eyes to break the contact between them. I put Voice into our newly created time frame.

We had experimented with this state of being earlier together with Terra, but now we appear to know more, and feel that we need to discuss our situation honestly, in a nonjudgmental environment, outside of human corruption. There comes an instant when every being chooses to commit or quit, to survive or die. This could be one of Voice's such moments. I face him with his own words and challenge him to explain.

Voice accepted my time shift as if it was natural for him. We immediately melded at a high level of brain and pidi interconnect. His basic human emotional need to compete with me fades, as Impulse conveys that there are no "challenges" from the human companion for Terra, the woman. Psychically, within this nebulous stopped time, we do admit this to him:

There is rational emotional desire for Terra, but the actions are for my love of Terra Firma, the planet. There's no challenge.

And then explain this to Voice:

Your words and music can help the planet's denizens evolve, change, and survive. Terra needs to be seen as the true embodiment of Mother Nature!

Conveying science and philosophy, we explain that Earth is merely a single cell in an organism that is an immense cosmos, with a brain far from the planet; Earth, an egg fertilized by special chemicals, irritated by others, and capable of surviving, no matter what exists on her surface or surrounds her. Only a cancerous bacteria on her surface can destroy her. She must choose to fight the irritation or die. Just like humans, she chooses to survive.

I explain to Voice with whom, and how, Impulse arrived to me, and include:

The technical operating systems in humans, such as brain, blood flow, nerves, chemical distribution, and more, replicate the systems in the body of the cosmos. To be as aware as your lyrics indicate that you are, you have an elaborate historical pidi attached to your current human being. We—you and I, Voice—have formed a very unique bond now, as deep as any humans attain, and on a galactic level.

Impulse then takes us on an intercosmos exploration—at the speed of nerves, surpassing the speed of light, and beyond human comprehension. As mere subatomic specks, we propel to the brain of the cosmos, and are charged by direct energy. Our pidis are filled with new and relevant data, spit back into the bloodstream on an instant path to the cancerous cell we need to cure.

Yes, I am an antibody, sent to find local healthy cells to help heal a dying body part, just like in humans. A cosmic antibody can love and communicate with humans when needed. A human brain has the power to comprehend a massive influx of new data, scientific facts, and experiences. It also has the ability to cure each individual cell within its mobility vessel, even if humans sometimes cannot accept it.

Time doesn't exist, and yet it is of the essence. Voice gets it, accepts it, embraces it. With the message conveyed clearly to Voice, we begin our mutual ascent toward the next phase of the solution, and head back to human earth time reality.

As we descend, Impulse chooses to ease up on the time stoppage, allowing the band to musically catch up to us in earthly time flow. We can hear the slow, dredging, guitar and bass riffs, and the slogging drums and colorful organ—all melded into a slow-motion backbeat calliope of blues-based hard rock music. Terra slowly sways to the music.

Newly enlightened by our cosmic exploration, Voice attempts to share his new knowledge, in order to effect positive change. He knows that he might be judged as crazy, according to human standards, but he is *compelled*, and can handle it, if it happens.

He sings his words, written prior to this recent trip through the stars, imparting love to the audience,

> "Dive like a mad man, a flying crying sad man,
> Circle the ground on wings of hope.
> Believe you can fly for as long as you can."

And, to compel others to recognize and allow their Hope beastie to overcome the Fear beastie, he sings,

> "Dive towards the crazy, the ultimate joy!
> Don't be lazy, or shy, or coy,
> Be the bird, not some beastie, in your mind,
> Discover the thrill as the sun burns your eyes,
> There is no awareness to tell you to stop,
> The ground comes ever closer to ending your drop."

Then, with all of his strength, surrounded by an army of happy positive beasties and his band, he sings a gut-wrenching,

> "You gotta DIVE!
> LEAP from the precipice
> Into the abyss!
> You gotta dive
> Like this!"

Vibe slides to the front center of the stage, offering a soaring, ethereal guitar solo. Merely hearing it burns the nerves with intensity, many consider joyous. As the music builds on this visceral chromatic crawl, the audience feels uneasy, but still steady and avid. They want to learn quicker and absorb faster than most of their unevolved brains' comprehension can allow. Voice knows this, and is kind. As Vibe raises the crowd to elation, Terra has turned away from her easel to watch Voice perform. I move downstage and join Voice,

> "Dive like the strong one, or some insipid wrong one,
> Watching your shadow on the earth below.
> The jump is your freedom, if you truly won."

Voice looks at Terra and continues,

> "Dive to the future! Your past is long gone.
> The open door of nature begs for your song,

See as those around you, in amazement, they watch,
The whole scene is changing to a world you can touch!"

Voice looks directly at the audience,

"It's all heading towards you, continue to fall;
There is only *you in your head* to answer your call."

He continues, conveying this emphatic plea for the audience to commit to change,

"You gotta DIVE!
Magic in motion!
Believe that you can!
You gotta DIVE!
Like I am!"

Vibe rips into the crowd again, shredding his guitar so tastefully, powerfully, that the audience will never forget this song, this moment. The crowd (practically in mass orgasm) breathes in heavy, slow unison to the rhythm created, anticipation and excitement growing (this currently being a total breeding ground for full-on chemical reactions!).

Terra's dancing with Voice in a way that undoubtedly represents the desires of all to mate! Voice leaves the dance and joins me downstage, singing,

"Dive like you know it's the best way to go!

Imagine what's good, and not what's down
below."

To which I respond,

"Your wings may evolve, but you've never
been here.
Feel the rush of the fall as you break the
air."

We coax the audience to soar with the music,

"Believe there's an option, the end is not
near.
It's all in your hands, your mind and you're
clear.
To dream big and hopeful, smile ear to ear.
Give change a chance!
Dive without Fear!"

Voice—oh, so soulfully!—sings,

"You gotta DIVE!
Leap from the precipice
Into the abyss!
You gotta dive
Like THIS!"

He digs in deep and lets loose with a guttural
cry,

"DIIIIIVE!
Leap from the precipice
Into the abyss!

You've gotta DIVE
LIKE THIS!
DIVE
LIKE THIS!"

And giving it all he's got with one last breath,

"DIIIIIVE!
DIIIIIVE!
LIKE THIS!"

Terra, obviously *totally* enamored by Voice, swings her hips to the groove as she stands at the easels. She's surrounded by happy beasties. She picks up two of the discarded protest posters, flips them over, and draws a large letter "Y" in the center of one, and large letters spelling "NOT" on the other.

Change matters...

Chapter Thirteen
"Why?"

Looking at the posters on the easels and sensing Terra's combined concern and adulation for Voice and the planet, I realize that I have done a lot on this project, but for some reason, completion doesn't feel eminent or certain. I perceive a shift but also feel that an explanation may be needed. At every turn, I feel like I'm beginning another chapter of this mystery. At least I have Voice as a companion on the path. And we both believe it's time to tell all to Terra.

When it comes to the history of human philosophy—the so-called questions of the universe, and the mysteries of life—science and fact sometimes "take a pass" for humans' speculation and irrational beliefs. It seems that conveyance of universal knowledge happens less when humans are closed-minded and believe there are only human designed answers.

And sometimes the actual answers, even though simple, are incomprehensible to the unevolved human mind, even if humans want to comprehend, or choose to believe in something their society or tribe doesn't want to be accepted. Change happens slowly on Earth, a concept also not easily understood by small minds controlled by fearful, hateful, or greedy beasties.

Terra has posed the proverbial human philosophical questions of all times, on her two easels, in front of all. The answers to the questions, "Why?" and "Why not?" have baffled all living organic matter since single-cell beings first decided to eat each other to survive, then decided to mate to propagate, then decided to divide and aggregate. Each decision was a Why?-or-Why not? supposition, which took an action to develop a solution. Terra is a barometer on the atmospheric temperature of an aggregated human spirit, undefined by conventional wisdom.

From the universal experimental perspective, humans are to the universe as single-cell bacteria on Earth are to humans. So, humans, merely a speck in size in a being the size of the cosmos, no one at a higher plane considers these questions, as the self-fulfilling body acts on improving the lives of *all* cells, atoms, tissues, nerves, ideas, and processes. Why *wouldn't* it, if it keeps the *whole* healthy?

The crowd continues to roar approval, and does it appear to have grown in size?

Voice glances at Terra. I stand next to her easels, eye-to-eye, unaware that she and I are locked in the same mental condition Voice and I had experienced. Terra's mind is open, and I encourage her to let out her concerns so that we can solve the problems of her namesake, Terra Firma. She conveys that she *needs* to know *all*. I let her know how much I love her as a human, and as a planet, and that her mate will always be *her* own choosing. I download important information from my pidi to hers via her eyes, and she understands what she must do.

Attuned to our psychic communication without reserve, Voice cues the band with a snap of his fingers. They kick into a funky number, and Terra moves confidently to front and center. Voice and I can see her beasties dancing with her, and the audience really digs the groove!

Moving to front center of the stage next to Voice, she sings,

> "*Why?* becomes the question,
> When answers are evolving,
> As the questions are asked,
> From many perspectives.
> Many options exist."

Voice responds with his astute lyrics (crafted years earlier, and now holding new meaning to him),

> "*Why not?* may be the solution,
> As there may be no correct answers;
> Each being only serves the purpose of
> moving time forward."

Terra adds,

> "And time never stops…"

To which Voice replies,

> "But that doesn't mean that anything is linear."

With the three of us fully in mental sync, I sing Voice's next verse explaining the universal perspective Impulse has given me,

> "Humans are the most curious of species,
> With traits of all beings that evolved before
> them,

Along with that special stardust embedded
within their genetic code.
They think, they feel, procreate, evolve,
manifest, and deviate,
Other species on the planet respect, fear,
and/or idolize."

Terra repeats,

"And time never stops…"

And Voice sings,

"But that doesn't mean that anything is
clearer."

The band shifts musical gears, changing the
tempo for my next vocal, helping to convey the
complexities of the human development of thought,

"Yet, there are some humans whose animal
instincts,
Internal grief, and conditioning, have made
them
Dangerous to the planet itself."

I move to the front of Dick T.Raitor's and his
trolls' slipshod, makeshift stage and point to the
campaign rally posters upon it advocating for gaining
more power and control.

"I have discovered, directly, in my face
The cause—perplexing the human race
On the planet—as the bigotry and hate,

Division, anger, fear, and greed were the same."

While the band blazes on, I stride to Voice and Terra at the easels, and throw my arms around them, just as if we were alone, and point out that...

"Curses that had destroyed previous universal experiments..."

Voice's and Terra's breathless response is,

"Yeah?"

As I continue, I portend that there are more violent ways to solve this global problem,

"Once a meteor was sent, instead of a messenger,
To restart this planet all over again."

Terra and Voice nod in approval,

"Uh-huh!"

And I conclude with this simple query about the destiny of mankind,

"Can humans evolve to be more than just a food chain?"

Terra slides downstage to the center and retakes up fronting the heavy groove, singing Voice's query about point of view,

"*Why?* could be an equation,
When answers are evolving,
As the questions are asked from many perspectives.
Many versions exist."

I know that Voice wrote this song at a time when he questioned his own self-worth, choosing to live instead of committing suicide when he believed he couldn't tame his bad beasties or find love. The words mean something else now, as he sings,

"*Why not?* can be deviation.
As there may be no correct answers;
Each being only serves the purpose to reproduce or die."

Terra and Voice harmonize this final sentiment,

"*Why?* is the big picture.
When answers are not coming,
As the questions are asked from many perspectives,
Many Universes exist!"

I chime in with the reality of everything from a cosmos frame of reference,

"And time never stops…"

Voice and Terra drift off with the music, singing,

"Never stops, never stops, never stops…"

Ethereally wrapping up the song musically, the band simmers allowing the dichotomy of song stopping and time continuing to bring the audience to an appreciative rousing cheer.

Time doesn't exist and that's okay with everyone on this beautiful day.

Chapter Fourteen
"The Price of a Kiss"

Voice is no stranger to fame, success, struggle, complexities, hard knocks, long grueling tours and, for his art, negotiating business with unscrupulous businesspeople. He has lived a life of experiences which have hardened him, and made him an apt spokesperson for a generation of music fans, literary scholars, scientists, and musicians. He epitomizes the meaning of being surrounded with good beasties, good vibrations, good aura, and the emanation of kindness and fairness.

Sure, Voice has had his bouts with his devils, as does every evolving being but, since he remains open-minded and able to change, he's a prime candidate for the accomplishment of his own mission, *and* to assist Impulse with his. I'm lucky to be able to be a small part of it all. And, not to mention the fact that his music and lyrics are truly inspiring.

But, with all of this global and universal drama going on, the man who is Voice—now aware of more than just his *own* personal perspective—wishes to communicate his appreciation of Terra to her in this song written to and about his affection for her. Here and now, in the concert, it is *the* right time to sing about this affection for Terra, in a song he wrote when he met her.

So, the band begins the introductory strains of one of my favorite of Voice's songs. It speaks of all humans' unrequited love, and the cost of finding the proper mate against all odds. Voice looks at Terra, then at the audience, and sings,

"I've come to consider, at a time like this,
The cost to a soul for the price of a kiss;
A futile desire for the simplest twist
Of nature's grace and human's bliss."

Voice is expressing, too, his disappointment in a previous relationship wherein he was the only one imparting any affection, and calmly laments,

"To crave, for a simple emotional lift,
A gesture, or words, an encouraging gift;
Instead to be burdening, creating a rift.
Time makes change the practical shift."

I grab the microphone acknowledging Voice's plight, as if it were mine, bringing the message,

"To dream, like a young man.
With the knowledge of the ages;
Like some stupid anagram,
Never know just who steps up,
Cuz anything can happen…"

And I give the chorus my emotional best shot,

"Giving back for graces earned,
Paying forward for lessons learned."

Vibe and the band riff on swirling melodies as Terra and Voice's beasties dance. The audience can see and sense the beasties among them—*and* onstage!—though, in their state of mind, most aren't sure if what they're seeing is real (and who can blame them?), but, this afternoon, reality is the farthest thing from anyone's mind. Vibe masterfully, musically enraptures the audience, the beasties, and the atmosphere to a unified state of pure flow. He nods to Voice that he's concluding his guitar solo. I notice that their silent communication, after many years of performing together, is practically imperceptible.

Voice smiles gratefully, and begins the second verse (commenting, really, on the fact that the beastie, Doubt, is long a part of his *unevolved* human experience),

> "Again, I consider the price of a kiss,
> When they are free everywhere,
> And can be had for an ask—
> Can this be discussed with mutual respect,
> Or best set aside for that moment when if?"

Terra brings her superb vocal prowess to the assertion that…

> "Imaginary reality is the kindest routine.
> Insecurity can destroy the strong dreamer's dream;
> Hopeless, it would seem, to believe that it's real;
> Must carve out time and space to heal."

I am telepathically keyed in on this fact: Terra knows that when Voice wrote those words when he was younger, when he was missing her company, her attention, her comfort; he was able to rise above the beasties, pain and fear, because his beasties, hope and love would overcome.

Time for some cosmic magic, Impulse relates to me.

We place Voice in the body and mind of when he was twenty years younger; and as he looks at Terra, he sings from his heart,

"To love like a young man…"

And I add my perspective,

"The universe guides me,
Like some fucked-up hologram."

Young Voice then sings,

"Never know just who will step up,
Cuz anything can happen!"

Terra, Young Voice, and I share a knowing look about today's cosmic trek when we stopped human-time. We're ready to impart to the masses' the solution to "life's conundrum":

"Giving back for lessons learned,
Paying forward for graces earned.
Giving back for lessons learned,
Paying forward for graces earned."

We repeat this over and over, and its rhythm becomes the heartbeat of the audience. I just know it can be heard as far as the concrete barriers at the edge of the Park forest, and heard high above the terrestrial plane! The numerous video cameras, phones and other electronic devices make sure it's felt by beasties all over the world. For some reason I just know it, feel it, and if we're getting it right, it would be felt throughout the nervous system of the entire *cosmos*!

Most importantly, though, it would be felt by Terra Firma. So that change can occur within human interaction for her health.

Just because Voice, Terra, the audience, and most of the beasties, are now evolving and attaining a form of happiness, doesn't mean that the message will reach *every*one. There are still those who choose not to evolve, choose not to learn, choose not to accept life's lessons, and choose to impart control on others.

As the band ends the song and the audience cheers, the beasties are overjoyed with elation!

Terra and I move to the easels from the center stage as Voice bows and accepts the adulation of an appreciative audience. She grabs another poster board and draws a large question mark that covers the whole board.

Next to it, I draw a U.S. dollar sign—a universally known symbol of the destruction of the planet.

Chapter Fifteen
"Foolish Old Man"

"All for one and one for all" were words one famous earthly author put into the mouths of three patriots. Now, as a unified force of spirit and will, we intend to confront evil and effect change (maybe via something read in a comic book, which could be one of the earth's best sources of inspiration in modern society). Books capture knowledge to allow future generations to evolve.

Change is not easy, but the only thing constant *is* change. At least, that was what one of the anti-pollution protestors' signs read. We now stand as humans helping Earth to stop small-minded monsters from destroying the life-giving atmosphere. The only way to save humanity is to save the living being, Terra Firma, and show her the respect that any woman deserves. Sure, the bad beastie-controlled humans control bombs, armies, intelligence, and laws, with their financial influence, but we have no choice but to try to help *them* change by opening their human minds.

Terra and Voice sang lyrical inspiration to the fans earlier, and it appears to have been successful— psychologically and scientifically motivating humans and beasties with a newfound open-minded ability for advanced processing of new and current intelligent data.

From where we're standing on the stage, we see that there are a lower number of bad beasties prevalent among Dick T.Raitor's former citizen supporters of his lies, greed, and corruption. They are *choosing* to change; their minds are now opened, their irrational beliefs have been eradicated, and they're willing to assist in saving planet Earth from annihilating humankind—the cancerous bacteria maligning the living cell.

But that's not gonna stop Dick T.Raitor and his miserably loyal trolls from their destructive desire to regress the planet, and profit while doing it. They snake their eely selves back to their makeshift platform and attempt, again, to explain why *their* way is the better way.

Voice cues the next song with a "Three, two, one!" and blasting through the loudspeakers come a guitar-bass-drums-organ onslaught which launches the next rocker anthem onto the crowd. Voice wrote this piece to shine a light on the lowest life forms scurrying in the undergrowth causing damage to Earth's roots, and of how foolish that can be. When the music starts, Dick T.Raitor mounts his platform and begins singing about his life, in another pathetic appeal to *any*one he can affect or corrupt.

The band is churning out rock n roll rhythms.

Impulse decides to take a moment to mentally bond with Dick T.Raitor to see if there is a light in his darkness. Pausing the evil beasties defending him from our presence, we want to take a few nanoseconds here and see what makes him tick. Dick's internal perspective of his life, success, and pain, shows a continuous stream of abuse from a narcissistic father who didn't know how to raise a child. This taught him that survival in a-new-era-of-global-change-for-domination is at the expense of *all others*, and that bullying, bribing, beating, and berating—accompanied by an arrogant, irrational core belief of *I can do no wrong*—he believes entitles him to deserve all he takes.

Dick T.Raitor leans toward his security detail and sings a corrupted version of Voice's lyrics,

> "I'm no foolish old man.
> I'll tell you what is real, or what's real in your mind,
> I'm the smartest old man,
> A younger man's dream in a well-worn mainframe,
> And the smoothest old man,
> Though no one can believe that this pretty girl is into me!"

Dick T.Raitor is gesturing toward a young female citizen standing next to him; she reacts with quite a questioning expression.

PunkHead then jumps onto the mainstage, stands next to Voice, points at Dick T.Raitor, and shouts,

> "Foolish old man!"

And Voice responds with,

> "He is just delusional!
> He's losing his facilities."

Dick T.Raitor continues his display of narcissistic arrogance, taunting the audience,

> "I'm such a clever old man with a checkered past!

No one could believe that my luck would
last,
As long as it has, never having to lose,
Wealthy and entitled, built a world I could
rule."

Hearing this honest dispersion, using Impulse's
teaching, it becomes our focus to point out to the
citizens Dick T.Raitor's weaknesses. I sing,

"A traumatized boy with no patience to
wait;
Within him bad beasties beyond human
restraint."

Voice adds,

"In between the agony, this humorless
beast"

And PunkHead joins in with,

"Can't be trusted to be kind, to say the
least."

Terra grabs a microphone and sings,

"He's a foolish old man!"

And the audience and the beasties all shout in
response,

"Foolish Old Man!"

Voice adds,

> "Not sure what is real, or what's real in his mind."

Dick T.Raitor's supporter-citizens defend him with,

> "He's no foolish old man!"

And the group of punk protestors call them out, screaming,

> "Foolish Old Man!"

Dick T.Raitor's arrogance is so evident in his next proclamation,

> "I'm a younger man's dream in a well-worn mainframe."

PunkHead, as snide as he can muster, sings,

> "Just a foolish old man!"

This causes PunkHead's people, and the rest of the audience, to chide Dick T.Raitor with another rousing,

> "FOOLISH OLD MAN!"

EarthaMom appears next to that young female citizen and sings,

"I can't believe that this pretty girl is really kinda into him."

In his own defense, Dick T.Raitor responds,

"I'm no foolish old man!
You are all delusional, and losing your facilities."

I move to the edge of the stage and face the beast Dick T.Raitor, and I sing,

"Hey, you foolish old man with a head way too large!
Why do you let all of this greed take charge?"

His response is predictably,

"My profit and fame are my true reward,
And none of it needs to be shared with the world."

I respond with what could be considered by rational humans with a reasonable question,

"Do you believe that you alone can decide all of their fates?"

And Voice sings his own lyrical question,

"Without science, conscience, morals, or a healthy debate?"

From his deeply clogged, subconscious hatred of himself, his past, and his detractors, Dick T.Raitor, with an over-inflated false bravado, declares,

> "I alone am the smartest, the greatest, the one,
> Who can keep the wheels turning and get the job done!"

PunkHead screams,

> "YOU'RE A FOOLISH OLD MAN!"

Now the *entire* audience responds with him,

> "FOOLISH OLD MAN!"

Dick T.Raitor's security detail paid to protect him and his ego, lean into a microphone to chide the audience,

> "Why don't you believe him?
> He's trying to do everything."

Dick T.Raitor sheepishly questions the audience with,

> "I'm no foolish old man?"

The audience, now including most of his former citizen supporters, shout,

> "FOOLISH OLD MAN!"

Dick T.Raitor sings,

"I'm just a younger man's dream;
That may be what you're looking for."

His few remaining supporters gathered on the platform shout,

"NOT A FOOLISH OLD MAN!"

And PunkHead bellows in response,

"FOOLISH OLD MAN!"

EarthaMom, still standing next to that female citizen, adds,

"That pretty girl was always just repulsed by him."

I sing with a laugh,

"What a foolish old man!"

And the audience calls back in response,

"FOOLISH OLD MAN!"

They are followed by Terra, adding the exclamation point,

"You are so delusional!
The sheep will turn away from you!"

Dick T.Raitor sees that these "mindless sheeple" he *thought* had accepted complacency as their new normal and would easily become subservient tools for his new society, are now resisting him. *Almost all* of the formerly supportive beasties surrounding their formerly brainwashed humans have *chosen* to change their perspectives with newly opened minds, therefore changing their *behaviors*!

PunkHead takes the lead, pointing at Dick T.Raitor with defiance,

> "You're not really a great capitalist!
> You're nothing more than a narcissist!"

The former supporter citizens (and the current batch still surrounding Dick T.Raitor's platform) ask in unison,

> "What happened to those promises
> To change the fate for the rest of us?"

EarthaMom sings,

> "He never meant *you*, Citizens!
> He was looking out for his brethren!"

Some confused citizens ask,

> "What about the families,
> Freedoms, and prosperity?"

Dick T.Raitor shrugs, and with his security and remaining staff in tow, tries to distract from the citizens' attack by awkwardly dancing a laughable attempt at dancing while throwing dollar bills in a randomly agitated fashion towards the audience.

PunkHead yells,

> "Hey, you foolish old man!
> We see through your scam!"

And Voice sings with call-to-action conviction,

> "Even those who had been fooled
> Realize that they've been had…"

Terra adds,

> "You had your time controlling our lives, for your plan…"

And I proudly proclaim,

> "Now the universe might try to take its own stand!"

The entire audience knows its cue and sings wholeheartedly,

> "FOOLISH OLD MAN!"

PunkHead, Terra, and I sing to Dick T.Raitor,

> "FOOLISH OLD MAN!"

Voice adds what everyone's thinking,

"Not sure what is real, or what's real in his mind."

And the crowd again responds, vociferously,

"FOOLISH OLD MAN!"

Now the punks and protestors scream,

"FOOLISH OLD MAN!"

Dick T.Raitor gestures as if surprised they are referring to him, admittedly singing,

> "I'm a younger man's dream in a decrepit old mainframe."

Terra points at Dick T.Raitor and sings,

"Foolish old man!"

And the audience responds in kind,

"Foolish old man!"

Dick T.Raitor begins to scream as he clutches his head and his chest, struggling to keep his balance as his *dancing* now appears to be more catastrophic.
EarthaMom sings the obvious,

> "Nobody believed that that pretty girl was into him!"

I shake my head in sorrow and sing as T.Raitor moans in the background,

"Foolish old man."

The crowd, in a rousing, change-of-heart chorus, proclaims,

"FOOLISH OLD MAN!"

Voice sings the lyrics he crafted detailing the reality of T.Raitor's life of excesses, the influence of that shallowness' importance in his mind, and the decrepit value it had,

"You are just as disposable as all of your commodities."

The music shifts eerily into a funeral dirge, a melodic peace, a calm, with a reverence to the universe, nature, and to humankind expressed in chords and aural semblance. The audience is overwhelmed by the emotions the music compels, as the beasties make their humans *feel* this feeling.

The power of love is now displayed in the words, the music, and on the art of *all* of the placards and posters! Flowers, peace signs, love hearts abound! There are no longer emblems of revolution, hate, bigotry, or corporate greed! I psychically communicate with Voice and Terra to assure them that there is some semblance of control and order in this scene:

Maybe this is only happening in this Park, on this day, at this time, but it is a moment in history that

those, standing right there, and affected worldwide, are truly feeling a change of heart.

The expression of this much goodwill causes the trolls to back away from Dick T.Raitor, as he stands alone atop his weakly-built precipice, occupying space that no longer desires him. The narcissism, hate, arrogance, and corruption beasties are angrily causing self-inflicted pain and pressure on his already weakened old body. The physical exertion of dancing created added strain on Dick T.Raitor's internal organs (what with his body *never* supported by any proper nutrients—his biochemicals, nerve responses, and basic bodily checks and balances within his human operating system are *all* awry).

Having bonded with Dick T.Raitor's being (as I had with Terra's and Voice's), we sense that, in his diminished condition, he is more open-minded and capable of connection. His mind and being are heretofore so *damaged* that cure is not possible. He's being eaten alive by generations of bad beasties growing within him, by being nurtured and sustained only by success at the expense of others, and by his learned and genetically inherited unethical and immoral beliefs.

I am deep within his subconscious, and able to tap into his pidi. I discover the sad truths beyond his current-being status. He once was an evolved and transcended being. His pidi shows me his history within the universal body, his voyages throughout the galaxy of nerves, his chemicals and systems that keep all aligned. When he and his pidi landed on Earth in this timeframe, he decided that he wanted to try another type of lifetime. *This* time, he would partake in all that would benefit *his* growth. He was led astray by humans. This allowed the bad beasties, which emerged during a lifetime, to negatively influence him—to set him on a path to *destroy* for his own fulfillment.

I absolutely sense that he has learned a lesson (it's recorded into his pidi for the future), but he's also fully expended his planetary life-giving energy (there is a finite time that a human being's bodily vessel can exist). In what appears to be a hope for reprieve, he telepathically attempts to convince me of his innocence in making these choices, but since I cannot give life to a human body, the attempt is futile—his bodily functions are expiring.

The human muscle that pumps the blood is a fragile organ and is not built for immortality. With the strain of his own bad beasties attacking his heart, and while his brain is unable to send proper chemicals to battle, the stress of this physical exertion takes its toll.

I know that Dick T.Raitor's heart has stopped pumping and, in front of the crowd he hoped to enamor, he's seeing, during his last breaths, their utter dislike for him. Deep in his mind, I sense his disappointment, but he's *still* arrogantly holding on to his irrational subconscious belief that he's been correct *all along*, and that the world will *not* do as well without him—a final narcissistic pat on his own back for what he delusionally believes. Sadly, I ponder that too many humans allow these bad beasties to drive them to an unpleasant demise.

In front of the entire audience, with the music playing, Dick T.Raitor clutches his chest, winces with pain, and struggles to remain in a standing position. His security detail continues to dance, holding him upright. T.Raitor stiffens, standing straight up, wide-eyed with surprise that this is happening, and cracks a wry smile. At this finale of this lifetime, his distorted perspective allows him to believe that they are all cheering *for* him. With that, his body goes lifelessly limp, and he falls into the arms of his security guards. The guards immediately toss Dick T.Raitor's body to the few remaining trolls, and—with complete and utter disregard—they abandon the tyrant T.Raitor's corpse.

The audience and band notice the activity on the platform; they all had pointed at Dick T.Raitor calling him out for his treachery, but not for his demise. I can sense that many feel that they may have caused his untimely passing with their bad beasties and negativity, and I recognize the shock from the crowd as, finally, his body is wrapped and dragged away.

But those who previously had supported him to power did not care or step up to empathetically feel for the loss of his being on the planet. They are now released from their need to support what they unconsciously felt was negative but was simultaneously perhaps in their best interests. They are liberated now.

I sense very *few* empathy beasties from anyone, except from Terra. Her belief is that every snake in the grass may just be a creature trying to survive the best way possible. She'd hoped Dick T.Raitor would discover his good beasties and change. To Terra, he may not have been able to recognize and reconcile the bad beasties within himself, but even the *worst* beasties, when they pass, are given graces by Mother Earth, and they once again become part of the planet.

I step up to the microphone to conclude this *scene* with a lesson for the crowd, who, conveyed with raw will and perseverance, brought down a cancerous evil in order to save the planet, and as a warning,

> "When that foolish old man was laid down
> in his grave,
> Natural causes the culprit from a life full of
> waste;
> There will be others following bad beasties'
> desire.
> To win by all means, set the planet on
> fire…"

Sometimes, even though their pidis remain full of all gained knowledge and experiences, beings may not evolve to a greater experience. In evolution, and in reincarnation, every being begins as a single-celled microbe or bacteria, and we all revert to the basics of chemistry and science when our physical presences are exhausted. Evolution is the growth each time we re-enter the universal system, wherever, or whenever, that is. Nothing wants to return again as a bacteria in a hostile environment— not when they have full knowledge of an alternative embedded in their pidi.

Like all humans immediately prior to the demise of their planetary mobility apparatus, Dick T.Raitor's last human thought in this iteration of his being, was the realization of being reintegrated into the earthly species hierarchy—as the larvae of a bug at a low evolutionary level and, in his pidi, all the DNA memories of his affluent and wasteful past life.

With this new technology prevalent among all of the people at this event, Dick T.Raitor's death onstage is captured by thousands, and immediately beamed worldwide through the electronic technology spanning the globe. All of the uneducated and brainwashed trolls of corporate profits and organized religion will need to find a new giant beastie to threaten the sheeple on their behalf (there are still *plenty* of humans who can only function in life, whilst guided by new false visionaries and false hope sellers).

I know that many of the righteously disillusioned citizens will return to their day-to-day lives, until told by their trusted, compromised, influenced, or brainwashed friends, family, and selective media, *what* to stand up for, or against. (I jumped ahead to the future there for you, so you could understand what happens to all those folks who need to just exist, who do not have imaginations, who need to just survive, who choose to believe that it's not them, that *it's always everyone else*).

The revolutionaries and protectors of the planet, who are against corporate and political corruption, and climate destruction, will find the next false icons to shine a bright light upon, when more bad beasties rise up to spread messages of greed, fear, and hate.

Dick T.Raitor... one bacteria eating at the planet, spurring others to emulate him... has been eradicated.

The aggregation of the good beasties of empathy, concern, kindness, and hope are all very visible to everyone who is paying attention.

Where is the love?

Chapter Sixteen
"You've Gotta Understand"

Voice and Terra have been attuned to my thoughts throughout this entire experience (we are, all three, unified). I am surprised by the evolution they both have attained in this short time here on Earth and, in the face of this situation, that Voice is staying completely calm and in control of his beasties. Here we three stand in front of tens of thousands of cheering humans, all attuned to Voice's lyrics and music, all accepting that all of his messages ring true, *and* that, with his guidance, good defeated evil (even if half of the attendees think it's merely a staged performance!).

In the uneasy ruckus that remains after witnessing the death of evil in the form of a human, the audience is unsure of how to react. Voice understands his place right here, right now, as written in the set list—he is to sing of his love for the universe, Terra, and Terra Firma. With a nod, again he cues Vibe to start the next song. It appears to be the time for all to know that the crisis may have passed, yet *can* recur. I walk to the easels and remove the placard with the meteor heading toward Earth, and toss it into a recycling bin just offstage, leaving the image of a heart alone on the easel.

Voice musters his strength and sings directly to Terra,

> "You may think that I don't love you,
> Or you may think I'm just a fool.
> I've just always had this trouble staying
> cool."

He gestures, then fixes his gaze directly at me,

"And when you've gone and left us
For some other memories,
Take the knowledge we've been humbled
and set free."

Voice and I sing to Terra, to the audience, to all
the beasties,

"You've gotta understand."

Then Voice sings sweetly to Terra,

"I'm just tryin' to be my own kind of man."

Voice and I harmonize a plea to her,

"You've gotta understand."

Voice takes Terra's hand and professes,

"I'm not useless, and I'm doing the best I
can."

I leave the easels and walk downstage center,
my eyes scanning this ocean of everyone. The crowd
stretches all the way to the concrete barriers! I
implore them all to be aware of what they take, do,
want, and believe, by singing Voice's lyrics,

"Do what you want.
Take what you need.

Leave what ya don't.
Don't soften;
Opportunity knocks just once,
But greed knocks often.
It can nail your coffin."

Voice and I emanate a plea to Terra, and the beasties that surround her,

"You've gotta understand."

And Voice lets her know,

"I'm just tryin' to be my own kind of man."

Voice and I proudly sing,

"You've gotta understand."

And Voice emanates his passion,

"I'm not helpless, and I'm doing the best I can."

Vibe joins us and plays a most magical guitar solo, musically capturing the positive spirit of this very moment—sheer elation created by music and good vibrations delivered via waves of energy and atmosphere interlocked, creating an unparalleled and unique experience for these humans (especially those further evolved).

We telepathically reach out to all present whose minds can grasp the greatness of this moment:

"A mass change in human behavior can occur when minds open, and irrational beliefs are replaced with knowledge, facts, science, empathy, love and kindness."

As Vibe concludes his mind-bending solo, the crowd is indeed enraptured! I sing to them,

"In your darkest moments,
I hope I brought you light."

Voice turns to Terra and sings of his lifetime commitment to mental well-being,

"Even as I grew up, keeping right…"

Voice and I sing to Terra about lessons learned throughout this epic moment in time, as the spirit of Young Voice joins the chorus,

"Remember all the good times!
Keep the spirit in your heart,
And always keep the heavens on your charts."

Voice, Terra, and I face the masses, singing proudly,

"You've gotta understand."

Voice sings with eternal optimism and patience,

"I'm just tryin' to be my own kind of man."

We onstage repeat our call for clemency for our past mistakes, growths, and bad beastie decisions,

"You've gotta understand."

Voice sings passionately to Terra,

"I'm not useless, and I'm doing the best I can."

He suddenly cries out to Terra, to me, and to the planet,

"You've gotta understand!
Gotta understand!
Baby, PLEASE!
Gotta UNDERSTAND, please!"

As Voice wails, he's surrounded by his good beasties (which are responding so happily, floating in unison above his head). The applause begins, builds, and peaks with a roar as Vibe completes the song with his masterful guitar.

To Voice, the sound of the masses' thunderous applause and cheering is a warm blanket on a cold winter night, wrapping Voice, Terra, and the band, in an aura of loving unity.

Did they understand?

There remains hope…

Chapter Seventeen
"Hope"

From the highest point of the tallest mountains on Earth, to the bottom of the deepest trenches in the darkest oceans, this planet holds the mysteries of life, often unfathomable to most humans existing in their proverbial time here (and who are controlled only by their pidi and pursuit of survival). The brain offers as equal a complexity as does the universe itself—and it offers the ability for *any* being, allowing itself to evolve, to see, and know *all*. The chemicals and organic systems in a human can also allow that human to understand and experience the depths, in their entirety, of the human spirit—via the acceptance of scientific fact, and applying the same to the current reality of the human's existence. The past is the past; if you did not learn, add to your pidi, and thereby evolve, then you may need to repeat the lessons until your evolution occurs.

It appears I was lucky enough on this day to have been *enlightened* to all of this with what initially appeared simply as an impulse.

I'm now being internally instructed that the most unpredictable and unique aspect of all humans evolving on this planet is the beastie, Hope. This element of behavior, thought, emotion, and action can affect people in both rational and irrational manners. The *hope* for anything can be a misleading exercise in futility, or it can be the only lifeline someone has for themselves and for their planet.

Terra is the ultimate representative of hope—in human form—that I have ever encountered. It may be because she also is a human form of Terra Firma, and representative of the complexities of this planet wishing only for the survival and happiness of all, including herself.

We have come to the last song of the set of which Terra is the featured vocalist, a musical work poetically stating her perspective and posing her questions. Voice cues the band, and Terra confesses,

> "I wake another morning at the dawning, lost in thought;
> Wonder about the thunder in my mind and in my heart.
> Moving to the future in the nurture of the pain,
> Alone with distant music, pounding rhythms in the rain;
> Human, yet immortal, lost in a time outside the portal,
> Given to disaster with a thought of dying faster."

As a messenger, I sing Voice's response to her universal query,

> "Hope can be fleeting,
> Never have the chance of being,
> The saving grace of knowledge and change.
> Be the one who inspires the sun,
> And blooms the flowers in springtime.
> Hope is the only magic that illuminates the strange."

Much to Voice's surprise, *Terra and I* sing the chorus,

"Give love to each other!
See the kindness of strangers.
Maybe Hope is the answer,
Whatever the question, can't be too kind,
Be kind to all!"

Voice casually (not possessively) takes Terra's hand and dances her away from me. During the musical interlude, as Voice and Terra dance together to secure their bond, I now am able to telepathically connect Impulse's pidi to everyone present (to educate quickly, and on a massive scale, is only able to be managed by our combined power). My co-pilot has evolved me to a point where my human system is now completely supportive.

Impulse poses en masse this psychometric question about the complexity of the human being, followed by answers in a massively complex data dump:

How can the human brain possibly function, chemically and psychologically, while mystically tied to every other living thing, and to the cosmos?

Open minds want the answer, and it quickly spills into them, demonstrating to me the possibility of science *proving* that the brain creates the beasties by writing its own internal script of beliefs and thoughts from external stimuli and influences, good and bad! The brain processes that information in a computer-like network of neurons, resembling what most humans before me now visualize as solar systems, just like in their night sky. Parallel with the nervous system channels, the brain can trigger an emotion—either imaginary or from memory—which sends a message to the hypothalamus, which sends chemicals through the bloodstream into the brain, thereby body-triggering beastie creation, good and bad.

These brain signals are also emitted beyond the internal human system and into the expanse of space known as the universe, and can be absorbed back from other sources. Many humans have evolved and developed their clairvoyant abilities, enabling communication with everyone and everything (using a *technology* that travels on waves *unknown* to *closed-minded* humans). Within every human with an open mind is the power to turn on this *switch*, as it is left in the *off* position within a closed, or compromised, human, wishing to remain unaware.

Inherent in this unique attribute (which keeps humans surviving against all odds) remains a belief, in the beastie, Hope, that *anyone* can choose to turn on the trigger needed to evolve into a better being. Unfortunately, too many humans waste away their beastie, Hope, expelling its positive energies, partaking in efforts of futility, encountering the discouraging experiences of waiting for another human, or a god, or a savior, or a deity, or a solution outside of one self's own evolution.

A human's acceptance of being part of a bigger universe, which may be as small as a single atom (humans may actually exist in a *sub*atomic scale), can never be fathomed by a defeatist. The beastie, Hope, wants to totally comprehend, chooses to explore, desires to learn more, and pushes humans on the path toward transcendence. The path to hope goes through the brain to reach the higher plain of existence.

Here on the stage, as the song moves on to the second verse, I release the audience's minds from the unified education session, just in time for them to cheer (yet again!) for Vibe's musical showmanship. He nods, acknowledging with self-confident pride, his love and appreciation of the fans and these most heartfelt accolades.

Terra sings the second verse which was written by Voice during a time of depression when he was deeply concerned about his beasties, his planet, and his love for Terra,

> "Another day of doubt, no idea what it's about,
> Isolation is not the equation to cure a human heart.
> Belief in the possible, and not the irrational;
> Learn what is feasible, even if it's difficult.
> The mind's the only muscle that can make you cry,
> And take you beyond the errant squandered wish to try."

I respond with Voice's lyrics about the power of the mind,

> "Hope may not help weaklings, or narcissistic beings,
> Working toward a solution to force their evolution.
> Power of the mind can create the kind of feelings
> Destructive to the soul—deep control of sad devotion."

The human psychological illness known as depression can be described as having a mind ensnared in what it feels is an inescapable trap, and the emotional frustration caused by a chemical distribution to the senses, which stimulates stagnation, and overcome with the desire to just give up trying. Sometimes the solution to a dilemma can be sitting in plain sight, and within reach, yet the unwillingness of the mind (due to human genetics or societal conditioning) to change the recurring inaction, causes the brain to continue to issue into your senses a flood of inappropriate chemicals. The situation is exacerbated by an acceptance of an "inevitable misunderstanding of life"—or by the irrational belief beastie, Arrogance.

As the song builds, the band is reprising their opening number, pointing to the audience and shouting,

> "What about YOU?
> And You? And You?"

As the music hits a mighty crescendo, Terra and I sing the chorus,

> "Give love to each other!
> See the kindness of strangers.
> Maybe Hope is the answer,
> Whatever the question.
> Can't be too kind.
> Be kind to all."

The band moves into another musical track with a psychedelic ethereal guitar, and I sing the answer to another big question,

> "Kindness is the currency, of the Universe,
> Spend freely... Spend freely."

Voice and Terra then reiterate for the audience some important messages imparted in this concert. First, they sing about the hopeful optimism from "Forever Girl,"

> "The rays of the sun are making shadows somewhere.
> It may be sunny here, but it's raining over there..."

After which they glean the kharma lessons from "Price of a Kiss," singing,

> "Giving back from lessons learned;
> Paying forward for graces earned."

To the crowd's joy, they conclude with an angelic,

> "Love and let love!"

Terra, with a newfound understanding of Voice's lyrics, sings about resilience and resolve,

> "Elation often fleeting leaves the heart slowly beating,

For the passage of time, or the change
within the mind.
As we witness the erosion of a soul
explosion creeping,
We find the strength to keep our distance-
length behind,
Moving with the wind, keeping a fluid
stance within the fire;
Never taking a chance to enjoy the
happenstance of desire."

Voice moves next to Terra, singing this to assure her that he shares her understanding of death and fear,

"Hope is a glance toward one happy dance,
against the odds,
Or there'll be nothing more than disaster in
store,
With only fear to follow."

I look to the audience and telepathically inform them:

Organized religion would take what was just sung, along with any advanced knowledge contrary to their teachings, and use it to control and weaken the human spirit with a false sense of hope, created only to empower and profit those who espouse it.

I then passionately sing Voice's next lines to hammer home my message,

"Believe in the outcome you want
Or find a path to your gods,

Lest your wishes and dreams become
Manipulated schemes of horror."

Everyone onstage—and all of the beasties of all
of the open-minded people who can now *see* and
hear—wholeheartedly chant with the band,

"Beasties, Beasties, Beasties, Beasties,
Beasties, Beasties, Beasties, Beasties,
Beasties, Beasties, Beasties."

The music swells, bringing everyone onstage
into a climax of musical momentum led by Terra
gracefully and emotionally singing alone,

"Empathy,
You see it in the floods and in the fires.
You see it in the hurricanes of human
desire…"

Now I lean in to join Terra to sing,

"Empathy,
You feel it in your panic to the cries.
Your actions show your feelings."

Voice joins Terra, and I to sing,

"As your spirit starts to rise."

Everyone present projects powerfully in
harmonic splendor,

"Empathy,

Drives you like an engine, deep inside,
To do what's right, no matter there's no prize."

The band stops on a dime, so that all the audience hears are the a cappella voices of Terra, Voice, and I as we sing,

"Give love to each other!
See the kindness of strangers.
Maybe hope is the answer,
Whatever the question, can't be too kind."

Everyone onstage is now gathered in the center, and the band winds down the rhythm to set up a finale styled kick-line musical expression. As we conclude the song, we want the message to be truly understood with the entire band singing,

"Be the Love for each other!
See the kindness of strangers.
Maybe Hope is the answer…"

Terra accentuating proudly proclaims,

"Be The Love!"

Everyone present sings,

"Hope is THE only answer.
Whatever the question!
Be kind to all!"

A beauteous mass of humans, a chemical reaction exuding amazing aural harmonies, sings,

"Be kind to all!
Be kind to all!"

Voice looks at Terra with a heartfelt smile of satisfaction. He then looks at me with a smile of pure acceptance, and everyone sings,

"Be kind,
Be kind,
To all!"

To conclude the finale, I reiterate our message which helped the beasties accept their fate, chanting,

"Unique is better than sameness!
Beasties, be kind!"

The song ends and the roar from the audience is tremendous. As a group of performers and entertainers, this band has succeeded in fulfilling their dreams, and are receiving the approval that they were seeking.

I now feel that this mission, this story, is nearing conclusion. Mystery morphs into fact; the lingering thought of, "What happens in the future?" becomes, "Where will this lead, and what can be expected?"

An unpredictable key to happiness is that the beastie, Hope, exists—whether delivered from some ancient alien, or some star-crossed lover, or some extraterrestrial visitor, or some religious icon, or is dreamt up by a disciple or a madman in order to control the weak-minded. *Hope* is the only universal message that all humans can understand, regardless of their distinctly unique personalities, discrepancies, and inadequacies (those differences of which are all delivered by a chemical concoction of genetics and environment, plus some unknowns thrown in to keep everyone guessing).

The question all beings have (which causes their internal beasties to become anxious, excited, or upset) is now answered and, with that, the message of *hope* has been delivered and received. The audience is fulfilled, and they react with overwhelming adoration for Voice, Terra, and the band.

I back away and head upstage. We're being removed from the focus of attention by my Impulse informing me to:

Let the energy be aimed at the band. We were just doing our part.

Time to go.

Chapter Eighteen
"I La La Love You, Goodbye!"

Done. Messages delivered.

My pidi tells me I've completed a level of the survival game. The planet now has enough aware humans to (possibly) correct the disease that was plaguing this shining experiment of the universe. Impulse now believes that he has succeeded in assisting me as well, with a sense of purpose and self-esteem that has been propped up by all of my good emotional beasties. I believe I have accomplished something truly positive to help the future of Terra Firma.

Impulse telepathically sings to me,

> *I la-la-love you, goodbye!*
> *I la-la-love you, goodbye-yi-yi!*
> *Ya didn't have to try;*
> *Ya wanna know why?*
> *I la-la-love you, goodbye!*

Then Impulse evokes everyone present to sing the *answer* to their experiences, in their turn, in real human time, and this is how it rolls:

Me and Impulse:
"I la-la-love you, so long!
I la-la-love you, so long-ong-ong!
Ya did nothin' wrong,
So I wrote ya this song!
I la-la-love you, so long!"

Ghost of Dick T.Raitor raps his response (appearing as a ghostly, holographic image): "Ya never saw a problem, or chose to change your pace,
So I'll kindly wish a fond farewell, and leave you to your space.
Though, every time you'll think of me, you might always hate my face,
Even so, I'll let you go, and even proudly say…"

Ghost of Dick T.Raitor:
"I la-la-love you, farewell!
I la-la-love you, farewell-ell-ell!
Wishin' you well—
Might see you in hell!
I la-la-love you, farewell!"

Voice:
"Ya wanna know what it means to be a real good friend?
Ya gotta dig down deep, and stay until the end.
Don't be too afraid, because the road has awful bends.
Even so, I'll let ya grow whatever way ya can!"

Voice:
"I la-la-love you, so long!
I la-la-love you, so long-ong-ong!
This message belongs in this simple song.
I la-la-love you, so long!"

PunkHead:

"Everyone is different, hard to compare.
You grew up hard and your folks weren't
there.
Mom was 'gone', and Dad didn't care…
Or Dad's unaware when Mom's on a tear…
Working, or playing, giving kids little care.
It wasn't our fault, just to make that clear!
Struggle in the bubble, so you're trapped in
fear;
Even though there are facts, fantasy's so
weird!"

And I sing:

"Livin' for the future is absurdly yet so near,
So I bid adieu, and give to you
The passage of some years."

Terra:

"Even though I haven't tried every which or
way,
There always seems to be an obstacle delay.
Happiness is fleeting, and sometimes goes
astray,
But if you don't try, and don't know why,
I'll have to truly say…"

Terra:

"I la-la-love you, goodbye!
I la-la-love you, goodbye-yi-yi!
Ya didn't have to try;
Ya wanna know why?
I la-la-love you, goodbye!"

The crowd cheers, sending a massive wave of positive energy—to the stage, beyond the stage, deep into the earth, and up into the stratosphere—literally shaking the concrete walls here *and* miles away.

A beam of light shines on me as Impulse reverses his arrival process on Earth and, using his pidi, attaches to that beam. I sense his departure from my body and being. I do not feel empty, or left alone, or even disappointed that he's gone. I am affected, I am changed, I am human and whole. I am now content knowing the secrets of the universe, and now *you* know them as well.

Planet Earth must look beautiful from afar, wherever that Impulse may have originated, from where we humans call outer space, or just our imagination… That beautiful atom, cell, egg, life form, microverse, woman, or however it's deemed in the imaginations of the universe, its poets, musicians, artists, authors, and dreamers.

I am thankful that I had an Impulse that day.

Epilogue
"Lessons"

You cannot lose what you cannot possess—just one of mother nature's tests.

Size doesn't matter, and time doesn't exist.

Kindness is the currency of the universe. Spend freely.

There are beasties within us all. Teach your beasties to be kind, respectful, and understanding in order to help make your universe a better place.